Guiding Fate

Tamra Lassiter

www.tamra.lassiter.com

Guiding Fate

Tamra Lassiter

Enjoy!

Tamra Lassiter

This is a work of fiction. Certain real locations are mentioned, however all names, characters, events and incidents described in this book are fictitious or a product of the author's imagination. Any resemblance to real persons, living or deceased, is entirely coincidental.

GUIDING FATE

Copyright © 2016 by Tamra Lassiter

ISBN-13: 978-1-942235-98-9 (trade paperback)
ISBN-13: 978-1-942235-99-6 (e-book)

www.tamralassiter.com

For Dicey June Kuhne

Chapter One

Melanie

I try to be a nice person and do the right thing, and what do I get?

Screwed.

When Deb asked me to watch Churchill, her English bulldog, this weekend, it seemed like such a fun thing to do. I knew Michael would love the opportunity, and it would show him how much work it can be to care for a dog.

"He's house-trained," Deb had said. *"He won't be any trouble at all."* That changed when Churchill had wiggled out of his collar and left me standing with his leash dangling from my hand.

He's a cute dog. On any other day, I'd be laughing

at the scene playing out before me. *Not today.*

Churchill walks quickly from bush to bush in my back yard sniffing the unfamiliar scents that a different part of town can offer. His snorts echo in the quiet darkness. He sounds more like a pig hunting truffles than a small dog trying to find the best place to pee.

Davidson, Virginia is a small town. How can the smells on my side of town be that much different than six blocks away at Deb's? Yet, here we are. I tiptoe around the yard trying to catch him, but he scoots away in quick bursts to elude capture.

"Churchill."

My whisper cuts through the quiet night. I watch through the light of the flashlight as he gives me a look that pretty much says *"Forget you, woman. I'll let you know when I'm finished her*e."

A snapping sound echoes in the night. I shine a wavering light into the darkness along the side of my small house. Nothing. *Thank you, God.* The sound could have been completely in my imagination—yet, goosebumps spread over the flesh of my arms. A tight curl of nervousness forms in my stomach.

Great.

It's almost midnight on a Friday night. I don't need this kind of stress in my life, especially after seeing Malcolm today. Is he here somewhere watching me? How long did he lurk in the parking lot waiting for me to come out of the hospital today? He knows the E.R. where I work is locked down, so he chose to ambush me outside. *Ambush*. That's what his visit felt like to me, although he certainly seemed more hopeful than that.

"Hi, Mel," he'd said softly as he stepped out from behind a van parked near my Taurus. Then he smiled, revealing yellowing teeth, as if the moment was some great reunion. If Malcolm was so interested in making a good impression, maybe he should have worn something nicer than baggy jeans and a crappy, old t-shirt. Maybe he should have taken the time to shave this morning. Truthfully, it didn't matter what he was wearing or whether he'd grown a beard a foot long.

What did he expect me to do, jump into his arms? *Not. Gonna. Happen.* He ruined his chances for that years ago when he left to pursue something more exciting than his pregnant wife.

I've never been one to keep my thoughts to myself, so when I saw Malcolm this evening, I'd told him exactly what I think of him. His expression had become harder and harder as I spoke until he'd simply held up his hand to me and said, *"Enough."*

"You stay away from us, or I'll call the police."

That's when his lips curved into a sinister smile.

My body convulses at the memory.

"Churchill, get back over here."

This time the dumb dog doesn't bother to even look at me. He scampers over to Miss Bunny's yard next door. At least I don't have to worry about Churchill waking her up. First of all, she's practically deaf, and second of all, she's in a rehabilitation center recovering from the fall she took last month.

Creeeeeek.

That sound was *not* my imagination.

What the heck was it? A vision of Malcolm settling into the lounge chair on my patio pops into my mind. Another jump as the adrenaline rush shoots through me. I spin around and shoot the flashlight beam in the direction of my house. Still nothing. I stand frozen in my spot as my breathing returns to almost normal.

Enough of this. I'm done with being annoyed and scared in my own back yard. I've had a long day at work, and if you combine that with the fact that my ex-husband is back in town, I'm done. This ends now. I march through the grass, my bare feet becoming quickly soaked with the dew. I keep the light focused on Churchill the entire time. He knows it's over. He stares at me with the same eyes Michael has when he knows his fun has come to an end.

My imagination has left me completely freaked out and stressed. I guess I'm not going to bed right away. I need a glass of wine and a...another noise. This time right behind me. I turn quickly.

A man.

Too tall to be Malcolm. He's too close.

My own scream rings in my ears as I bring my flashlight around quickly, connecting with the man's head. He falls to the ground.

A mixture of adrenaline and dread pump through

me.

Who is he?

What did he plan to do with me?

Run.

I rush back across the yard and into the back door of my house. My shaky fingers turn the lock. The tears have already started falling. My breaths border on hyperventilating. I grab my cell phone off the counter and dial 9-1-1 as I run for the stairs, taking them two at a time.

I have to check on Michael.

"9-1-1. What's your emergency?"

"Hold on."

I throw open the door to Michael's bedroom.

He's there in bed sleeping peacefully, despite my rushing into his bedroom and the drama unfolding around us.

"Ma'am. Are you injured?"

I back out of his bedroom and close the door quietly behind me.

"Um. No. I'm okay."

The calm, steady voice on the line snaps me out of my panic. I'm a nurse. I should be ashamed of myself for overreacting the way I did outside. But then, I can handle the crises of other people much better than my own.

I tiptoe back downstairs to my kitchen as I give the woman on the phone all the details of my encounter. I decline her offer to stay on the line with me. I need to call Kate. By the time I disconnect the call, my adrenaline rush is calming.

That man didn't belong in Bunny's back yard, but he hadn't threatened me or tried to harm me. He was just standing there. *Crap.* Did he intend to hurt me? Did I overreact? I need to make another call.

Kate answers on the third ring.

"Mel, what's wrong?" A good assumption, since I'm calling her at midnight.

"I'm okay, but I need Hunter. Can he come over?"

"Of course. What happened?"

"There was a man in the back yard, and I hit him with my flashlight and knocked him out."

"Are you okay? Did he hurt you?"

My moment of calm is over. I'm panicking again. I hear muffled sounds as Kate tells her husband what's happening. "The police are coming, but I could use Hunter, too. Please hurry."

"We're on the way. Stay on the phone with me." This time, I'm happy for the company.

Churchill barks at the back door. Now he wants to come inside? Stupid dog. I take a long look through the window. When I don't see any impending danger, I quickly let him inside and again lock the back door.

In minutes, two police cars are in my driveway with their lights flashing. I watch out the window as the beams of their flashlights bob toward the back yard of my neighbor's house. Churchill, who's been lying on the kitchen floor, bounds to the back door and begins barking.

"You better not wake up Michael. Do you understand me?"

Churchill stops barking, sits on his hind legs, and looks up at me with wide, innocent eyes. He cocks his head to the side as if to say, *"Who? Moi?"*

What the hell is wrong with me? We've been dog-sitting for less than five hours, and I'm already conversing with the animal.

Using the door and my leg, I block Churchill from getting outside as I peek out toward the policemen. The kitchen lights prevent me from seeing anything in the darkness. I slide through the small opening and close the door behind me.

The flashlight beam is focused on a man. He's awake. He sits in the grass rubbing his head. The policemen standing nearby are conversing with him, but I can't make out any of the words. I hug my arms around my middle and tiptoe closer. My bare feet again make contact with the wet grass.

An ambulance arrives, the siren blaring and lights flashing. They cut both as soon as they park out on the street in front of my house. I'm sure every one of my neighbors is awake now. *Please let Michael sleep through this.* That's who I worry about the most. He's a heavy sleeper, and his bedroom light is still off, so maybe there's a chance.

I move closer.

"William Everton," he says in a deep voice. "I'm staying here."

My knees weaken at his words. *This is not good.* I swallow hard and dredge up the courage to ask the question I already know the answer to.

"You're Bunny's nephew, Will?" His eyes lock with mine, hard as steel. "What..." A nervous sigh escapes. "What are you doing here?"

"Technically, I'm Bunny's great-nephew. I'm staying in Aunt Bunny's house for a bit while she's in the rehab hospital."

One of the policemen turns his attention to me. It's Bryce Chambers. Bryce is recently out of college and one of the newer additions to the force. I know all the policemen in town. There aren't many of them in Davidson, and I've had occasion to work with them from time to time when they accompany patients into the emergency room where I work. To top that off, my best friend, Kate, is married to one of them, so I see them sometimes socially as well.

"Melanie, you okay?"

I study the man whom I thought was such a threat. He looks considerably different now. He did look scary in the dark night. Of course, anyone would have looked menacing after the thoughts I was having about being ambushed again by Malcolm.

Will is tall—I can tell that much even though he's sitting on the ground. Tall is scary, right? *Geez.* He's sitting in the wet grass. The dampness has probably soaked through his jeans. That's the least of my problems right now because I know who he is. He wasn't trespassing in Miss Bunny's back yard.

I was.

The dizziness and nausea hit hard. Sweat breaks out all over my body despite the cool temperature. *Deep breaths.* My nurse training tells me that's what I should do, but it's not enough to correct the fact that I assaulted a man in his back yard, at least his aunt's back yard. I'm the one at fault.

"Melanie?"

Bryce is next to me now. His voice is full of concern as he reaches out to support my elbow. His warm touch provides enough comfort for me to gather my thoughts.

Words finally come to me. "I'm so sorry. You startled me. I thought you were going to hurt me."

"This was partially my fault. I heard noises outside and saw someone walking around with a flashlight, so I came outside to make sure he wasn't up to no good. I saw the dog when I got back here. I shouldn't have gotten so close to you without speaking. I just wanted to get a good look at you myself to assess the situation, and it's so dark out here, I couldn't see a thing."

"My floodlight is burned out."

The EMTs, Joyce Crawford and Matt Foster, rush up to our group. This keeps getting better and better. Now, even more people I work with know that I assaulted my neighbor. Joyce kneels down next to

Will and slips a blood pressure cuff onto his arm.

"Melanie, would it be okay if we go into your house to ask you a few questions?" Bryce asks.

I'm going to be questioned.

By the police.

Will seems to have a good attitude right now, but what do I do if he presses charges? Could I go to jail? Surely not. *Please don't let me go to jail.*

"Sure," I manage to squeak out the word.

I don't take my eyes off of Will until Bryce turns me in the direction of my house. We walk toward the light shining from my kitchen window like a beacon guiding me to safety. Only, I might not actually be safe. Bryce is going to question me about the assault. I'm not the type of person who hurts others, especially physically. But, what if Will really had been an attacker? I'd done the best I could with the information I had at the time. Bunny's house was supposed to be empty. It was dark except for the couple lamps she usually keeps on, and the man was standing right behind me. He'd scared me to death, and I was already on edge, thinking Malcolm could be out there in the bushes somewhere. Would I have reacted that way if I hadn't seen Malcolm earlier today? He's the reason I'd worked myself into a tizzy.

Churchill is right at the door, waiting for me to return. With a quick bark, he hurls himself at Bryce before he even makes it all the way into the house. Bryce closes the door behind us, takes a few steps into the kitchen, and kneels down to pet Churchill properly. Churchill immediately rolls onto his back, giving Bryce complete access to his tummy.

"This whole thing wouldn't have happened if you had stayed in my yard, you big dummy."

My censure does nothing to change the look of pure contentment on Churchill's face. He opens his mouth and lets his tongue hang out to the side.

I grab my jacket off the back of the kitchen chair and put it on over my nightshirt. Besides the fact that I need some coverage over what is basically a very long t-shirt, I'm suddenly freezing. I zip up the jacket and hug my elbows to me.

There's a soft knock on the back door. I look up in time to see Kate push the door open. She rushes to me and pulls me into a tight hug. For the first time since this ordeal started, my eyes moisten. I let the tears fall.

Chapter Two

Will

My headaches are usually bad enough on their own without a crazy woman whacking me on the head with her flashlight. It couldn't be a plastic one, could it? Nope, it had to be the big, honkin' industrial model.

But there was something about the look on her face when she learned who I was. Even with the goose egg that was growing out the side of my head, I had to let her off the hook. She looked so vulnerable standing there in the cold, barefooted in her nightshirt. I thought for a second she might faint. Officer Chambers seemed to have the same thought as he went rushing to her side and then walked her into her house and out of the cold.

The darkness had kept me from getting a decent look at her last night, but that didn't stop my mind from filling in the blanks in my dreams. She was in all of them. Her chestnut brown hair. Because I hadn't been able to make out their color in the dark, those eyes of hers changed color each time I imagined them. Maybe a medium blue or a light brown? Definitely something in the middle. In every dream she was there, speaking to me in her honey-filled voice and wearing that pink nightshirt. I had focused on her face when I'd met her last night, the shock and the sadness in her expression. Apparently, my body remembers the look of her breasts, even through her shirt, because that vision played over and over as well.

Bells ring out and echo through the house. I immediately grab my head to stave off the pain. If I'm going to live here for any length of time, I'm going to have to lower the volume on the doorbell. That ear-shattering sound might be necessary for Aunt Bunny, who's half deaf, but it's not going to work for me. I make a mental note to add that job to the growing list of odds and ends that I've noticed since my arrival yesterday. I don't bother to get up off the couch. Whoever it is will move on. They aren't here to see me, and I'm not in any mood to speak to anyone anyway.

The bell rings again. A moan escapes this time as the pain shoots from the middle of my forehead down my back to the tip of my spine.

Please go away.

The bell chimes yet again. The pain crescendo rushes down from my head and ends in a wave of nausea at my empty stomach. Take a hint already.

This has to stop.

I roll off the couch, push myself onto my feet, and trudge toward the front door. I'd like to move faster to ensure the doorbell doesn't ring a fourth time, but each step gives me a jab of pain in my head. The nausea rolls around a little more. Finally, I'm at the door. I wrench it open, and I'm forced to close my eyes to ward off the bright sunshine.

Geez, why did I get off the couch? Having the doorbell pierce my skull would have been better than the pain now throbbing in my head.

"What?" is all I manage to say. The harsh tone conveyed in only this one word surprises even me.

The silence goes on for a couple beats.

"Um." It's *her* voice. I open my eyes enough to squint at her.

Light brown—that's the color of her eyes. The unfussy word doesn't convey how special they are. I need another word...caramel? That's better. She studies me without speaking. She's standing on my porch, which I guess I shouldn't be that surprised about after what happened last night.

Her hair is a deep brown just like in my dreams. It falls past her shoulders onto her purple t-shirt. Her cinnamon scent fills my nose and battles with the acid in my stomach. I let out a long sigh and lean my head against the doorjamb.

"I'm Melanie Woodside, by the way. I thought I should come by and say hello after the mess last night. Please accept my apology. I'm really sorry about what happened." She blinks a couple times, showing off the longest eyelashes I've ever seen. Have I ever noticed a woman's eyelashes before? I register the thought before my brain goes back to pounding. I really need to lie back down.

"It's fine."

"But you're not—fine, I mean. We need to get you to a doctor." She steps closer and reaches her hand toward my forehead. I lean back, the small movement enough to ring my ears. "I'm a nurse. You need to let me take a look at you."

"No."

"You shouldn't have declined medical treatment last night. I could have really hurt you."

"You didn't do this. You should go."

She stands a little taller. I notice for the first time that she's holding something in her hands—a plate with foil on top.

"I'll leave. I just wanted to apologize in person and bring you these." She gestures toward me with the plate. "Cinnamon crumble muffins."

So that's the cinnamon smell, not her. My stomach jerks again as if protesting food of any kind. I can't do this anymore. I close the door.

Chapter Three

Melanie

Watching Michael play with Churchill this weekend and listening to his laughter—the deep, belly laughs —makes me wonder if it would be worth all the work that comes with pet ownership.

Churchill's on his leash now. I've tightened his collar one notch to avoid any issues. After the incident last night, I'm not taking any chances.

My gaze moves over to Miss Bunny's house. Will's in there. I can feel it, even though there isn't a car in the driveway. How was I supposed to know someone was staying in Bunny's house? I've been gathering her mail and watching the place since she fell and broke her hip. I visited her on Wednesday in the rehab center. She didn't mention that anyone was coming to stay with her. How was I supposed to know?

Bunny speaks of Will often. I know a lot about him, actually. He's single and lives in Florida at the moment. He's a Marine. Well, he was last I'd heard. I know he was injured in the line of duty. Bunny hasn't told me all the details, but I know he's been on medical leave for the last couple months. He gets debilitating migraines. I'm sure that's what was happening earlier this afternoon when I went by to bring him my peace offering.

What I said to Will was true. I wanted to apologize to him for overreacting and thank him for not pressing charges. I'm a good person who can't go to jail. I have a son to raise. Now, I feel like I need to apologize again for bothering him when he was in the middle of a migraine. Apologize for apologizing. I don't dare do that, though. I don't want to take the chance that I would catch him at a bad time and have the door slammed in my face again. But, it's hard thinking of him in that house alone, suffering. Maybe I didn't cause his headache in the first place, but I'm sure my blow to his head didn't help.

A large and long sigh escapes me. His health and loneliness are not the only reasons I'm thinking of him. Will is hot—as in *Hot* with a capital *H*. How anyone can look that good in a t-shirt and sweatpants is beyond me. I'm sure it has something to do with the tight chest and muscular arms that fight against the soft fabric of his shirt. It could also be his eyes, which are somehow a combination of a deep blue and brown. Two eye colors that don't normally go together, but somehow mix to show the depth of his soul...and his pain.

We round the corner of the house into the back yard. Churchill runs a circle around Michael, wrapping his leash around his legs. Michael falls and laughs. Churchill runs his big, pink tongue up Michael's cheek. I can barely make out their movements in the twilight. Michael squeals with laughter and throws his arms around the dog so that Churchill can lick him some more. Yeah, I'm definitely going to have to reconsider our dog situation.

I hear an audible click as I step onto the patio. The area is suddenly bathed in light.

My floodlight.

It's back in operation. But, how did this happen? And when?

I pull out my phone and text Kate. Hunter might be responsible. He's a nice guy and Kate might have asked him as a favor to her.

My floodlight is fixed. Did Hunter do it?

She quickly texts back.

No. He planned to do it tomorrow since he had to work today. Maybe it was your dad?

In the past, I've changed the bulb myself. It's just one of those jobs I put off because it's a pain to haul the ladder around the house from the garage. Plus, I'm not exactly a fan of heights. *Hmmm.* Dad hates ladders more than I do, which is why I hadn't asked him to do the job. I hadn't even mentioned to him and Mom that the burned out light was a factor in what happened last night. I spoke about the incident as if it wasn't a big deal, so they wouldn't worry. I couldn't *not* mention it. Word gets around in this small town. That's the same reason that I had to tell them about Malcolm being back. It's better that my parents hear this bad news from me first, so I can play it down. My mother would turn into a raving lunatic if she heard the whole story—that the police had to come to my house because I'd beaten someone up with a flashlight.

I look again toward Bunny's house. There are more lights on inside the house tonight. The television's on, too. Could it have been Will who replaced the light bulb? If so, his condition had changed a lot since this morning if he managed to climb up on a ladder sometime this afternoon. It had to have been when Michael and I went to Minnie's Diner for dinner. We were home the rest of the day. Will could have easily seen us leave.

Is doing my home repair the likely action of someone who had practically slammed the door in my face?

Sunday brings a crisp fall morning, possibly crisper than it should be for the middle of October. I don't mind though; fall is my favorite season. I love everything about it: pumpkins, mums, hayrides, apples, and Halloween. I've always loved the season, and even more so since this is the month Michael was born. His birthday is on the twenty-fourth.

My baby will be five this year. It's crazy to imagine that he could possibly be that old. It was a tumultuous time in my life with Malcolm leaving me while I was pregnant with our baby, but then Michael was born. He was the best gift I could have ever received and exactly what I needed to snap out of my depression. There's no time to wallow in self-pity when you have a baby who needs you, and you're the only one there to care for him.

Look at Michael now. He's sitting on the front steps talking to Churchill and explaining that even though his owners will be here soon to get him, we will come and visit. Right on cue, Deb and Harry pull into our small driveway and park behind my blue Taurus. Churchill lets out a loud bark but doesn't leave Michael's side until his parents are right next to him.

Thank you for that, Churchill. Michael would have been devastated if Churchill wanted to go home too badly. We help Churchill get settled in the back seat of Deb's car. After lots of goodbye kisses and promises to visit soon, Deb and Harry are able to pull out of the driveway and head home.

Michael's eyes immediately well up with tears.

"How about we stop by the store and get hot dogs and baked beans for dinner tonight?" Michael's favorite and not a meal that he gets to eat very often.

"Really Mom?"

"Sure. It's a good day for grilling, don't you think?" Just like that, he smiles. I chastise myself briefly for using food to improve Michael's mood, but it doesn't happen often, and it's been a long weekend already, even though it's only Sunday morning.

"Can we get dessert?"

"Sure. Maybe some yummy strawberries."

Michael purses his lips and brings his hands up to his hips. "Maybe strawberry shortcake?"

Geez. My child is negotiating at four. He lifts his eyebrow and smiles. Where did this come from? If he learned this tactic in preschool, what kind of shenanigans can I expect when he gets older? I give in.

"Fine. Why don't you grab the card you made for Miss Bunny, and we'll stop by to visit her on our way to the store?"

Michael's smile grows even bigger. He rushes into the house and back in record time.

Bunny Everton has lived in Davidson her whole life. She grew up in a house one street over, met the love of her life, Jimmy, on her first day of elementary school, and then moved into this house when they got married the summer after their high school graduation. If this were the only information you knew about Bunny, you'd think she lived a simple life, but truthfully, there's far more to her story.

Jimmy volunteered to serve in the army during World War II right after their wedding. Bunny worked in a sheet metal factory in Richmond while he was deployed. After the war, they raised a son and a daughter. She has five grandchildren, and two great-grandchildren. Miss Bunny knows the names and birthdays of every single one of them. She's lived alone in the house next to me since Jimmy died more than ten years ago.

Her children, Billy and Julie, went to college in California, got jobs out there after graduation, got married, and never came back to Davidson to live. With the exception of a granddaughter in Memphis, her family lives out west. They've tried to get Bunny to move closer. She won't hear of it. Sure, she flies out there for a long visit now and then, but she insists that her home is here. She says she can't imagine leaving the area where she and Jimmy spent their lives together.

Bunny and I have coffee together a couple times a week. She helped me immensely when Malcolm left. Kate was living in Texas then, so I leaned on

Bunny probably more than I should have. My parents helped me a lot during that time, and Kate did too, but it was nice having someone to talk to who hadn't known me my whole life.

She's slowed down some in the last couple of years but only slightly. She slipped in her bathroom last month and broke her hip. Her surgery was successful, but her rehab is taking a while. Bunny entered the Patterson Rehabilitation Center at the end of September. I go by and check on her when I can after one of my shifts at the hospital and usually once over the weekend.

Michael and I say hello to Maddy, the receptionist, and head down the hall to Bunny's room. I pause the moment I hear his voice. *Will is in there*. Michael tugs on my hand, and I let myself be pulled into the room. I can't explain to Michael why I don't want to see Will, but this is likely to be a very awkward experience. I paste on my best smile as we round the corner into the room.

I keep my gaze focused on Bunny. She looks really good today. Her light gray hair has been "done," and she's wearing a hint of make-up. She's dressed in pants and a button-down blouse and cardigan—her usual outfit. It's nice to see her out of bed. She does still have bad days when she doesn't want to move much, so seeing her making an effort is fabulous. Maybe having Will in town is the extra push she needs.

"Look who it is," she says excitedly.

Michael drops my hand and goes in for a hug. He proudly hands over the card he made for her.

"This is you." Michael points to a bunny that he drew on the cover. He almost always depicts Bunny as a bunny. He thinks it's the cleverest thing ever that she's named after an animal. I tried to explain once that *Bunny* is a nickname, but he didn't want to hear it. "This is Churchill."

"Who's Churchill?" Bunny asks in an excited and patient tone that only grandmother types seem to use.

"We babysat him this weekend for Mommy's friend. I wish you could have met him. He had to go home this morning."

"Maybe he can come back for a visit when I get home."

Michael's expression brightens. I try to keep my focus on Michael and Bunny. I haven't looked at Will yet, but I do have to. He's sitting right there next to them. I sneak a peek and immediately wish I hadn't. How can sitting in a chair look so good?

Will's showered and cleaned himself up since the scruffy version I saw of him yesterday. He wears jeans and a button-down, plaid shirt. He's also shaved, revealing an angular chin. He sits up straight in his chair and gives me a polite smile, showing off perfect white teeth and little wrinkles in the corners of his eyes. He turns to my son.

"Hi there. I'm Will. You must be Michael. Aunt Bunny's told me an awful lot about you, and I've seen your fine artwork hanging in her kitchen."

Will offers his hand to Michael for a shake. Michael stares at Will's face and then at his outstretched hand. He lifts his little hand and confidently shakes with Will.

"Who are you?"

"Michael, that isn't polite." Even if it is a fair question. It would have been nice if I'd known the answer on Friday night.

Will shoots me a smile. "I'm Bunny's great-nephew. My grandmother was Bunny's older sister."

"That's cool. I don't have any aunts or uncles. Mommy is the only kid in her family, and I'm the only kid in my family."

Will looks up at me. I shrug my shoulders. What am I supposed to do, apologize for being an only child and then only having one child of my own? I planned to have more than one child when I married. I just thought I'd stay married a lot longer than I did.

"Mommy, do you know Will?"

My throat suddenly feels tight, but I manage to answer. "I do, Sweetie. We met on Friday night when I took Churchill outside before bedtime."

I bite down on my lip to stave off the heat I feel emanating from my face. I should have pulled Michael away from the door and figured out any way possible not to come into this room.

Chapter Four

Will

She's doing it again—chewing on her lip and looking at me with those intense eyes. The movement brings a stirring in my middle. I'm the last thing any woman needs right now but especially a woman like Melanie. She clearly has too much on her plate already with working full-time and raising Michael by herself. She doesn't need me to look after, too. Still, I can't reason my way out of being attracted to her. She's beautiful. Any red-blooded male would be affected by her.

I stand and step toward her. She doesn't move away, but she does fold her arms in front of her chest as if requiring some type of protection from me. I don't like it.

"I'm sorry I was so rude to you yesterday when you came by. I had a monster headache, but that's no excuse for how I behaved."

"Is that why you replaced my lightbulb?"

A quick intake of breath gives me away. I did replace the bulb when she and Michael were out yesterday. I didn't think she would figure out it was me so quickly.

"I did that for my own protection. I wanted to save myself from any future poundings."

What was meant to elicit a smile totally backfires. Melanie's shoulders slump, and her eyes water. She takes a deep breath and stands ramrod straight.

"You didn't have to do that. I'm perfectly capable of changing the bulb myself."

Uh-oh.

"I never said you weren't. I just wanted to do something nice for you since I treated you so badly when you came by yesterday morning. You don't have to get all wrapped around the axle about it."

She blows out a curt sigh and turns to Bunny. "Michael, let's get going, honey. We have to get to the store."

"So soon?" Bunny chimes in now.

"You just got here." I put my hand on her shoulder and get the response I was looking for. Melanie's eyes meet mine. "I'll go."

She swallows heavily. "No, you don't have to do

that. We really can't stay, anyway. Michael only wanted to bring Bunny his picture." She steps away from me now and closer to Aunt Bunny. She leans over and gives Aunt Bunny a careful hug. "Glad you're looking so well today. Call me if you need anything." Melanie grabs Michael's hand and pulls him out of the room, only giving him time for a quick goodbye. She doesn't look back.

"What did you do to Melanie?" Aunt Bunny's admonishment takes me by surprise.

I don't answer right away. Instead, I let out a huge sigh and take my original seat next to her, feeling the disapproval of her stare the whole time.

"We haven't had the best of luck with each other so far. I told you already about how she clubbed me in the head the other night." We'd just covered that story before Melanie and Michael came in. "Yesterday, she came over with muffins, but her visit was right in the middle of one of my raging headaches. I shouldn't have gone to the door in the first place, but she kept ringing the bell and didn't leave me a choice." I had barely gotten the door closed before I hurled on the mat. Aunt Bunny tilts her head. "I felt bad about my behavior, so I replaced the burned-out bulb on her back floodlight. I thought that was a nice thing to do for her. I never meant for my assistance to be construed as a sign of Melanie's incompetence. Of course she can change a lightbulb."

"What was that crack about how you were trying

to protect yourself from more beatings?"

"That was a joke," I fire back. "I was trying to lighten the mood."

Aunt Bunny shakes her head. "How did that work for you?"

Another sigh. "Not good, obviously. What do I do now?"

"Go to her door and apologize like a man. That's much better than sneaking around and doing home repairs when she isn't looking."

"Melanie isn't innocent in this either. She's the one who whacked me on the head in the first place. I let her off easy. I didn't press charges even though she did the assaulting, and we were both in your yard when she did it."

"You go over to Melanie's house and apologize the second you get home. I love that girl like family. You need to treat her the same way."

"Yes, ma'am."

Clearly there's no arguing with Aunt Bunny.

I rehearse my apology as I drive back to Aunt Bunny's house. The truth is that I'm not sorry for having replaced the light bulb. Why should I have to be sorry? It was a nice gesture. Plus, I already apologized to Melanie about being rude to her yesterday. Look where that got me. This sucks.

The sun shines brightly as I pull my pickup into

the darkness of Aunt Bunny's garage. It barely fits next to Aunt Bunny's huge Caddy. Uncle Jimmy added a bay to this tiny garage years ago so she wouldn't have any trouble parking inside. I don't even go inside the house. Instead, I walk out the garage door and hang a left turn onto the grass. Melanie's Taurus is in the driveway. I know she's home, so I may as well get this over with.

I study her house as I walk over. It's smaller than Aunt Bunny's but still has two stories. It's covered in pale yellow aluminum siding and has white trim. Black shutters line the front windows. There's no porch, but there is a small awning to shelter the oversized, brick front stoop. It's the perfect starter home for a small family. Is that what Melanie and her husband thought when they'd bought this place?

Melanie sees me through the long window beside the door before she opens it. Her eyes widen slightly at first, but she wears a smile on her face when she opens the door. How can she be surprised to see me? Did she think that display of annoyance in Aunt Bunny's room would keep me away? Hardly.

"Hi, Will. What can I do for you?"

Let's just get this over with.

"I want to apologize again for the way I behaved yesterday and for basically everything I've done and said since the first time I saw you Friday night. I'm not sure how we got off on the wrong foot. I'd like to start over."

Melanie opens her mouth to speak, but no words

come out. She sighs. "I'm sorry, too."

"Okay. Then let's make this official. We never did actually introduce ourselves." I hold my hand out in front of me. "I'm Will Everton. I'm going to be staying at Bunny's for a while."

She clasps my hand hesitantly. "Melanie Woodside."

Her caramel eyes are soft and warm. Her hand is soft and warm as well, but I force myself to let go when I should.

"It's very nice to meet you, Melanie."

"You too, Will."

She smiles but doesn't say another word. She doesn't invite me inside either. This is about as far as I got during my practice rounds in the car on the way here.

This conversation—if you can even call it that—is getting awkward. I should leave. Instead, I stare into her eyes a little longer. I don't want to go.

Melanie's gaze travels over my shoulder. The color drains from her face. I turn to see what has brought about this abrupt change.

A silver BMW slows and comes to a stop near her mailbox. The passenger window is rolled down, allowing a clear shot of the driver. He appears to be around thirty with black hair and dark eyes. He wears a smirk that I read more as a warning than a greeting. He nods his head in our direction and drives away.

"Who's that?"

Melanie bites her lip, clearly uncomfortable. Maybe I misinterpreted the gesture earlier at the rehab center. If this is Melanie's tell that she's upset, maybe it doesn't convey the meaning I'd hoped.

"No one to worry about."

She's lying, of course. If the fact wasn't obvious by the inflection of her voice, the shakiness of her hands gives her away. Melanie folds her arms across her chest and clears her throat.

"I realize we just met, but I'm right next door if you ever need anything."

Cup of sugar. A fist to pound someone.

"That's very nice of you." Her tone is all politeness. "I'm going to go check on Michael now. Thanks for stopping by."

"I mean it."

Her eyes meet mine. "I know."

She opens her front door and walks back into the house. The lock clicks as I see the same car driving past again in the opposite direction. I stand tall and don't break eye contact with the mystery man until he's past Melanie's house, and he has to look away.

Chapter Five

Melanie

I feel eyes on me again, as if people are staring. This hospital is like a second home to me. I've always felt comfortable here.

Until today.

Is it just because people are talking about me and the mix-up with Will on Friday night? Is it because Malcolm's back in town? I choose to blame Malcolm. He's the reason I was so paranoid on Friday night in the first place.

I bring the gurney carrying Mr. Henderson to a stop in the hallway right outside of x-ray.

"Mr. Henderson, Matt, the x-ray technician will be right out to see you." I give the elderly man a pat on the hand. "I'll see you back in the ER soon."

Mr. Henderson gives me a smile despite the pain he must be feeling from his likely broken leg. Poor man. He lives alone and fell in his kitchen this morning. Now, he's afraid that his family won't let him live alone anymore. I didn't know Mr. Henderson before he came into the ER this morning, but we've spent a lot of time getting to know each other. He's a sweetie. Fortunately, our hospital here in Davidson is small and usually quiet, so I'm able to spend some time talking to our patients. I've heard that isn't the way it goes in bigger hospitals, which is another reason I love living in Davidson so much.

I slip into the inner x-ray office and wave to Matt. He's on the phone, so I slip Mr. Henderson's order into Matt's inbox. Everything is computerized in our hospital, but I still bring a paper copy of the order with me when I come here. Old habits die hard, I guess.

With a quick goodbye wave to Mr. Henderson, I head back toward the ER. There's no one in this hallway, and yet I still feel like someone's watching me. Paranoia is becoming a habit for me. I feel eyes on me everywhere. Earlier today, I felt I was being watched while at the nurse's station. It wasn't Malcolm. It was only Ellen. She's a co-worker who happened to be looking in my direction while daydreaming. She smiled an innocent smile when she saw me staring back and looked dutifully embarrassed. Besides, a lot of co-workers have stared at me today. Word of my *mishap* with the flashlight last Friday night was all anyone could talk about this morning when I came to work.

I haven't seen Malcolm since he drove past the house yesterday, but I still feel the effects of that visit. Hence, the paranoia.

How embarrassing was it that Will had to be there at that moment to see Malcolm's display of testosterone? How many times has Malcolm driven by when I haven't been outside to see him?

Bunny knows about all the history between Malcolm and me. She lived it right along with me and was there to help me pick up the pieces when he left. I do have other people in my life I can count on, but my best friend, Kate, was in Texas then, so I could only talk to her on the telephone. It was Bunny who would invite me over for coffee and hold me while I cried.

Mom and Dad weren't so helpful when Malcolm first left. They didn't blame me for his departure, and while they've been here for me and Michael in countless ways, they just can't seem to fathom the idea that Malcolm left me. They couldn't help but ask *why*. I didn't have answers for any of their questions, of course.

I don't understand it myself, really. Sure, I've rationalized that Malcolm's a selfish person and didn't want to be tied down with a family. Geez, looking back, I don't think he really wanted to be married all that much in the first place. He probably would have left me eventually, but when I told him I was pregnant, he left within days.

Our marriage wasn't perfect. I knew that. There had been little clues here and there, but I rationalized them all away. Deep down, I think I knew Malcolm wouldn't be thrilled about being a father. I didn't let myself actually think about it enough to come to that conclusion, but I knew. Things are clearer when you're looking back on history from the present.

A really big sign: I waited more than a week to tell Malcolm about the pregnancy. I jumped for joy when those two blue lines appeared on that little white stick. I was so nervous about taking the test that I couldn't sleep and finally got out of bed at four o'clock in the morning to get it over with, for better or worse. I danced around the bathroom by myself in complete silence so as not to wake Malcolm. I hid the test under the vanity and pretended that day was just like every other day while I tried to think of a cute and clever way to tell Malcolm the news. That's what I told myself at the time, anyway. In reality, I was buying time. It wasn't long before the weight of the news became so heavy, I knew I had to tell him.

The dinner I made was perfect. Roasted leg of lamb—Malcolm's favorite meal. I almost threw up twice during the preparation just thinking about the fact that I was cooking lamb. Yep, I already had the queasy stomach. But I persevered, and in the end, it was a stunning presentation. The table was beautiful with a sapphire-colored tablecloth we'd gotten as a wedding gift and had never used. I lit candles and everything.

Malcolm was on guard as soon as he came through the door. He studied the table for a moment and then watched me closely as I buzzed around the kitchen. I smiled as innocently as I could. Another big clue. I wasn't feeling excited for the big surprise. I was worried. I didn't see that then, but it's clear as day now.

Malcolm was working on a lawn-mowing crew then. He came in from work and went straight to the bathroom to get cleaned up. When he came into the kitchen to grab a beer, I leaned in for a hello kiss. Malcolm did not. He looked at me for a moment before turning away and walking over to the television.

That's okay, I thought. He's had a long day. That was me then, always letting Malcolm off the hook. We'd only been married for five months at that time, and I was already in the habit of making excuses for his insensitive behavior.

Malcolm was quiet during dinner. I made nervous chitchat as we ate. Malcolm gave one word answers only when prompted. I revealed the big news during our dessert—homemade cheesecake, another of his favorites.

"I have some wonderful news," I paused for dramatic effect and to swallow down the hints of

nausea that had formed in my stomach. I smiled a huge smile. *"I'm pregnant."*

First, the color drained from Malcolm's face. He stared back at me with thoughtful eyes, although what he was thinking, I had no idea. Next, the color came back into his face and not in a good way. His cheeks flamed with anger.

"How could you let this happen?"

Me?

How could *I* let this happen? Not exactly the response I had been looking for. Malcolm was supposed to look at me with loving eyes and then call his parents to give them the great news.

None of that happened.

"I was hoping you'd be happy. We're going to have a baby."

"Do I look happy?" Not at all. *"You can, you know, take care of the problem."*

"An abortion? Absolutely not. You're talking about our baby."

The resolute indignation in Malcolm's expression makes my stomach lurch even now. His reaction was a flashing light that told me in no uncertain terms that he was not the man for me.

He stood up and walked out the door, and I told myself that he needed some time to warm up to the idea. That was all. I was still making excuses for him, and I kept telling myself that story for the next three days until he left for good.

I wipe a stray tear that threatens to fall. *No way.* I

won't allow myself to cry one more tear over my sorry ex-husband. I had cried enough in the months that led up to Michael's birth. I was alone and full of hormones. It was a tearful time. Since then, I've grown stronger, and my opinion of Malcolm has changed. He's the last person I want in our lives right now or ever. Having him back in town is the last thing I need.

Malcolm has no rights to Michael. I made sure of that in the divorce. Looking back now, that's one good thing that a quickie divorce did for us. Malcolm no longer wanted any part of me or Michael. He demanded that stipulation in the divorce, which I readily accepted. If Malcolm is now having second thoughts, well too bad for him. He can shove his thoughts of parenthood where the sun doesn't shine.

I turn a corner to see Kate's parents walking toward me. Grace is usually easy to spot in a crowd. For starters, her hair is a bright silver that's the envy of many people her age. She keeps it cut short in a very stylish bob. Plus, she's usually wearing some type of bedazzled ensemble honoring Elvis. I don't really understand her fascination with the man, but I give her points for not caring what other people think and wearing whatever she wants.

Today, she sports black pants with an aqua cardigan over a white t-shirt with Elvis's face outlined in black. Several silver bangle bracelets circle her wrist. She's one of the few people I know over the age of thirty who can wear a fan t-shirt and have it come off looking fashionable.

Albert's wearing dark jeans and a button-down flannel shirt. That's pretty much what he wears most fall and winter days. Dressing is so much easier for men.

Grace is such a great mother. She's supportive and understanding—two traits that my own mother doesn't always follow through with, even if she does mean well.

Grace's eyes widen when she first makes eye contact. She looks away quickly.

"Hi, Grace. Hi, Albert. What a nice surprise." I try to keep my words upbeat because it's clear that they aren't here for a good reason. Of course, this is a hospital, so other than visiting a new baby, there aren't many happy reasons for being here.

Grace's hands clasp together. I study her more closely. She's pale, like really pale.

"Is everything okay? Do you need to sit down?"

"Oh, no. I'm okay." She exchanges a look with Albert. Some kind of communication passes between them. Albert shuffles his feet.

"I'll go ahead and get the car. That'll give you two a chance to talk." Without another word, Albert continues down the hall behind me.

"I know where we can talk."

Grace says nothing in reply. I take her by the arm and guide her toward the ER. I have two active cases that I can't skip out on, but there are a few quiet corners where we can discuss what's going on here.

Whatever's happening is clearly serious.

I badge us inside and exhale a quick sigh of relief when I see my name hasn't been added to any new cases on the station board. It's Monday afternoon, not exactly a hot time for accidents, thank goodness.

I escort Grace into an empty patient room and close the door. The lounge is an option, but we could be interrupted in there. This will be quieter. We sit down side by side in the two chairs beside the bed. I scoot mine around so I can face her. Grace's eyes show her worry. She doesn't speak immediately, so after several long seconds, I prompt her.

"How bad is it?"

She sighs heavily. "We just got out of meeting with Dr. Hanover." She pauses there, knowing what the mention of Dr. Hanover's name means—cancer. I reach across the void between us, take her hand, and squeeze. She squeezes back tightly. "It's ovarian cancer. We weren't sure if it was cancer or not, but the biopsy confirmed it. He just gave us the results."

"What treatment does Dr. Hanover recommend?"

"I have to have a hysterectomy followed up by chemo or some type of targeted therapy. They'll know more after the surgery, once they determine if the cancer has spread outside my ovaries. He said I have a very good chance, actually."

"Cancer isn't something to be messed with, but there have been a lot of advancements with the treatments."

"That's what Dr. Hanover said. He also said that

since I'm healthy otherwise, my chances of beating it are even better."

"When's your surgery?"

"In two weeks."

"Does Kate or Brady know?"

I already know the answer because if Kate knew, she would have talked to me about this. And if Kate's brother, Brady, knew, he'd have told Kate. There aren't many secrets between them.

Grace shakes her head. "I didn't want to burden the kids without knowing for sure."

I nod. "I understand that, but you're going to tell them, right?"

"Yes, of course."

Big sigh. Tears are in her eyes, and seeing them makes my own eyes moisten. "Please don't worry too much about this. It's a setback, sure, but you've always been a tough one, Grace. You're going to kick cancer's butt. You know that, don't you?"

She manages a small smile. "Yeah. I won't go out without a fight." I pull her to me for a hug. "You won't tell Kate about this, will you?"

I lean back and look her in the eye. "Of course not. This is your news to tell. She'll be pissed if you wait too long though. You'll tell Kate and Brady soon, right?"

"Definitely. I don't want to risk Kate's wrath."

Chapter Six

Will

"Long night, sweetheart?"

Is it that obvious? Last night was particularly bad. The lack of sleep led to another migraine. I waited until this afternoon for my visit, giving the pain time to subside.

Aunt Bunny sits up a little straighter in her chair and studies me with concerned eyes. One look at her, and maybe I'm the one who should be concerned. If the bags under her eyes didn't give her away, her appearance certainly would. She's wearing sweatpants, a t-shirt, and slippers. Aunt Bunny wears a long nightgown to sleep in, so while I know she got dressed today, she still opted for comfort over looks. I've come to see her every day that I've been in Davidson, and I've never seen her look so comfortable. She always wears slacks and a real blouse or a sweater. Her long gray hair is always fixed nicely in some kind of bun. Not today. It falls down loosely over her shoulders.

"It was kind of a long night. How about you?"

She shrugs. "I just couldn't seem to get comfortable. So I didn't sleep much."

"Why don't you take a nap?"

"I don't want to mess up my sleep cycle. This happens sometimes. If I can stay awake until dinner, then I'll be able to sleep through the night."

"They can give you something to help you sleep."

"Probably, but I don't want to take it."

I lean over, kiss her on the head, and take a seat in the chair next to hers.

"You are as stubborn as a mule."

"It takes one to know one."

Her quip catches me off guard. A chuckle escapes. "What did I do?"

Bunny's mouth forms a thin line. "You know what I'm talking about." She tilts her head, her eyes practically boring a hole in my skull.

"Do you mean Melanie?"

"Of course I mean Melanie, you twit." Bunny's not very subtle when she needs sleep. "Have you talked to her?"

"I went and saw her on Sunday, just like you told me to. I apologized. We're starting over."

"Well, have you seen her since?"

"I've seen her." It's true.

Big sigh from Aunt Bunny. She leans toward me. "Don't get smart with me, young man. Have you talked with her?"

"No, but I haven't had the opportunity."

"You need to make the opportunity. The two of you are perfect for each other. You both need something good in your lives."

"Aunt Bunny, I'm not perfect for anyone right now. I'm a mess."

"Tsk. Tsk." She actually says the words out loud as she shakes her head. "I think you'd be good for Melanie, and she would be good for you."

"How can you say that?"

"Because it's true. She hasn't been with anyone since her ex-husband left."

"Michael's father?" She nods. "How long has he been gone?"

"Since before Michael was born. Malcolm found out Melanie was pregnant and took off." My mouth drops open. Bunny nods and then shrugs. "Melanie was a mess."

"What was he like, her ex?"

"Nothing special. They moved into the house right after they got married. Melanie has such a sweet soul. I took to her right away. She was so excited about being married and making their new house a home. I could tell Malcolm didn't feel the same way. I was nice to him for Melanie's sake, but I never liked the man. One time, not long before he left, I caught him in my garage."

"What do you mean?"

"I came home from the grocery store and pulled my car into the garage. I had bought my next-door-neighbor on the other side, Pearl Livingston, some pecans. They were on sale, and I knew she'd want them for making pies." *Get to the point.* Aunt Bunny must read minds because she finally does. "I left my garage open while I walked over to Pearl's house. When I came back, I found Malcolm standing in my garage looking at me."

"What did he say?"

"At first he didn't say anything. He looked like a cat in a room full of rocking chairs. He looked around nervously, saw the groceries in my open trunk, and made up the excuse that he saw me come home and wondered if I needed help carrying the bags into the house."

I nod, and Aunt Bunny goes on.

"I very clearly told him *no thank you*, and he left."

"Did you ever find out what he was doing?"

"Yes. I'd left a twenty dollar bill on the table to help me remember to take it by the Methodist church for a fundraiser they were doing. The bill was gone. I never came up with anything else that was missing."

"What did Melanie say when you told her?"

"I never did tell her, and I didn't call the police. I don't want Melanie to ever know about that incident. Malcolm left her about a week after that. She blames herself for being dumb enough to marry someone who couldn't handle family life. I didn't want her to know he was a criminal on top of that."

"Were you scared? You know, when you were alone with him, and he looked so nervous?"

"No. At the time, I was fuming mad. It wasn't until later that I thought about what could have happened. I didn't think Malcolm was a violent man, but then, once he went to prison..."

Wait. What?

"Malcolm was in prison? For what?"

"Armed robbery."

"Poor Melanie. She must have gone through so much."

"She has, which is why I say she needs some good in her life. You both do. Why not find a little happiness with each other?"

"It's not that simple."

"You care about Melanie already, don't you?"

Our eyes meet, and I can tell. She knows I like Melanie. How does she know?

"It doesn't matter. I'm no good for her in my current condition."

"So you've said. You'd better be careful though. You're only in town for so long. You don't want to waste all your time in Davidson coming to see me when you could be spending it with Melanie."

"Why am I here? Why did you ask me to come?"

"I needed someone to watch after my house."

"Melanie was taking care of everything—not that there's much to do right now other than get your mail and water the plants on your porch. Julie told me that you made her go home after the surgery. What can I do for you that your own daughter can't?"

"She's bossy, and you know it. I couldn't take her telling me what to do all the time. That's my job, and you know it." Aunt Bunny chuckles.

"Julie said you made them all promise to stay away until you were out of this place and home again. Why do you want me here, and why now?"

"I thought it would be good for both of us." She places her hand on mine. Her skin feels cool to the touch. "You know you've always been as close to me as any of my grandchildren. The truth is, I've really missed you. I haven't seen you since your parents' anniversary party, and that was almost three years ago. You haven't been here to visit in more than six years. I know it was hard to get away when you were deployed so much. You always loved coming here when you were younger, so I thought the change in scenery might do you some good."

A sigh escapes. I guess coming here has done some good. I'm no longer writing only about my nightmare in Iraq. My time this week has been much more happily spent, writing everything I know about Melanie. I don't know as much as I'd like to know about her. Much of my journaling centers around her scent, her hair, and the lightness I feel when I'm near her. I've filled dozens of journals since the incident—frantically writing at first, and then less and less frantic as I work through the pain. This is the first time I can remember where most of my notebook has logged happy thoughts.

Bunny squeezes my hand, bringing me out of my thoughts. "I think you're right. A change of scenery is a good thing."

"Of course it is."

"Hi." Michael's little voice practically echoes in the twilight. I look up to see him waving enthusiastically from their driveway. I wave back. I had heard Melanie's car pull in. I focused on staring down at the tabletop and not at her and Michael. I wrote in my notebook for as long as I could until twilight set in, and even with the porch light, I couldn't see well enough to continue. It's been fully dark for at least an hour now, and I continued to sit out here. The cool air feels good.

"Mom says you'll hurt your eyes if you try to read in the dark."

I look up to see Michael standing at the bottom of the steps. He'd make a good soldier with his quiet advance across the grass. Of course, his size makes it easy for him to be sneaky, I'm sure.

"Your mom's right."

I close the notebook and look at the little boy

who's now made his way up the steps to stand next to the small wrought iron table where I sit.

"Michael, please leave Will alone, honey. You can't just run over here and bother him."

"I'm not bothering him."

I feel both of their gazes on me. Michael silently urges me to back him up. Melanie does the same.

"Your mom's right about that, too." Michael's face falls. "You're not bothering me, of course. I mean the part about you running over here. You should always ask your mom if it's okay to leave your yard."

Melanie lifts her eyebrow to let Michael know she means business. She walks up the steps until she's on the porch as well. She's wearing navy blue scrubs under her jacket. Her eyes are tired. I move to stand up. She places her hand on my shoulder to stop me. I feel the warmth through my sweatshirt and t-shirt and down into my chest.

"You don't need to get up. Sorry that we bothered you, Will."

"It's no bother. It's nice to see you."

Michael's expression brightens.

"See, Mommy. Will likes to see us."

"Okay, mister. Let's go. Time for bed."

Michael looks at me again. I shrug my shoulders at the injustice of the world. He sighs and walks back down the stairs. Melanie squeezes my shoulder as she turns her body toward me, flashes me a conspiratorial smile, and mouths "thank you."

Then all too soon, she lets go and follows Michael

down the steps.

"Goodnight, Will."

And just like that, those two minutes were the best moments of my day.

Chapter Seven

Melanie

My smile grows even bigger when I'm hit by the scent of apple pie. Mom's apple pie is the best. It's exactly what I need after a long day at the hospital, especially today. Gloria Nelson came into the emergency room this afternoon with dehydration caused by severe diarrhea. Let's just say it was awful and leave it at that.

"Mommy!"

Little arms wrap around my waist. I allow my eyes to close as a sigh escapes. This boy is everything to me. I plop down into a kitchen chair and pull Michael onto my lap.

"Tell me all about your day. Did Miss Megan like

the marbles you brought in for *things that start with the letter M-day*?"

"She did. I'm glad I picked marbles instead of Mister Moose because Trevor brought in a moose. I don't want to be the same as him."

Michael's smile grows a bit bigger at his good fortune. The truth is, he almost made me late for work this morning as he ran around the house looking for something to bring to class other than his moose stuffed animal. He'd worried it might look too babyish to bring a stuffed animal in to school.

"We had baked chicken for dinner. Can you eat some here before you go home?" Mom joins us in the kitchen. Her short, gray hair sticks up a little on the very top, probably from playing with Michael. The messy hair goes perfectly with her comfy powder blue sweatpants and matching sweatshirt. She looks at me expectantly with those calming blue eyes of hers. "It's Friday night, and there's no school tomorrow. No need to rush home."

"Sure, that would be great, Mom."

Michael cheers and rushes into the family room. The sound of the television is loud enough that I can tell Dad is watching a football game.

Mom sets a dinner plate in front of me. As promised, there's baked chicken with mashed potatoes and green beans.

"This looks delicious. Thank you."

She sits down in the seat across from me. "You're welcome, sweetie."

I take a big bite of chicken and swipe it through the mashed potatoes for extra flavor. Delicious.

"Any word from Malcolm?"

Odd question.

"What kind of word? I haven't seen him all week. I sincerely hope he's left town."

"He hasn't."

What? How would Mom know that...unless?

"Did you see him?"

Mom looks down at her lap, where I can tell by the set of her shoulders that her fingers are clenched together. She gathers herself and then makes eye contact.

"He came by today to see your father and me."

"Malcolm came here? Why on earth would he do that? Did you let him in?"

Mom's mouth curves into a nervous smile. "He just wanted to say *hello* and let us know that he's back in town. Of course, everyone knows he's back in town. I've had five different people call to tell me that they've run into him this week."

"What did he really want?"

"He apologized to us for leaving you and Michael like he did."

"You didn't let him off the hook, did you?"

Mom's forehead furrows. "Of course not. But..." Oh no, there's a *but*. "It has been five years. People do change as they mature. You two got married awfully young."

"I was twenty-four. Malcolm was twenty-six. That

isn't too young, Mom. Don't make excuses for him. Malcolm made his choice, and he's not getting another chance."

"I don't expect you to forgive him easily, but maybe you should listen to his side of things and see what he has to say. You were in love once. Maybe you can remember what you loved about him. He certainly still loves you and Michael. Maybe in time you can give him another chance."

The few bites of dinner I've had churn in my stomach. I can scarcely believe what my mother is saying right now.

"Did he put you up to this?"

"Of course not."

I stop short of saying *Of course he did.* Maybe he didn't. Maybe this stems from Mom's desire to have the perfect family. It was painful for her, too, when Malcolm left. She wants a cozy, happy life for her only child, and she really wants more grandchildren.

"You know Malcolm was in jail, right? Did he explain that?"

"Your father asked him about that. Malcolm admitted it straight away. He didn't try to hide it."

My stomach churns some more. I take a deep breath to calm myself. I can hardly believe I'm having this conversation. "He had to admit it. He was convicted of armed robbery."

"He said that it was a big mistake. He was lost after he left you and was running with the wrong crowd. He didn't know his new friends were going to rob that gas station."

That's what he said in court. I wasn't there, but I did research the hell out of Malcolm's trial. That's why the jury only gave Malcolm two years in prison. The other men involved were sentenced to more time. I take yet another deep breath to help keep my voice down. Michael shouldn't hear any of this conversation.

"Do you hear yourself? You're asking me, your only daughter, to consider taking back a convicted felon who left me when I was pregnant?"

Mom sighs. "Well, when you put it like that..." My eyes widen. *Seriously?* "Malcolm was so sincere with his apologies. I never understood why he left in the first place. The only explanation is that he was having some kind of mid-life crisis, and he couldn't handle a family. He's grown up and certainly ready for one now."

Mid-life crisis? The man was twenty-six, for goodness sake. I stand and walk my mostly untouched plate to the counter next to the sink.

"I'm too exhausted to have this discussion right now, Mom. We're leaving."

She stands and gives me a warm hug. I let her. She's my mom, and she's doing what she thinks is best for me—well, maybe in some bizarre alternate universe. Here I go again. Am I making excuses for Mom now? Bringing Malcolm back into our lives isn't the best thing for anyone, especially not Michael. She has to see that. She should've kicked him off the property the moment she saw him.

She releases me, and we walk together into the family room. Michael's cuddled up next to Dad on the couch, both of them intently watching the game. Where Mom has fair hair, skin and light blue eyes, Dad is more like me. Well, I guess I'm more like him, and so is Michael. They have the same brown hair and the same light brown eyes. They look like two peas in a pod, sitting there on the couch together.

Neither looks at us until I finally speak, "All right there buddy, time to go home."

"Papa said I can watch football with him."

Dad smiles and tilts his head. "I said we could watch football until your mom was ready to leave. Sounds like she's ready to leave now." Michael's face immediately falls, and with it, Dad's smile. "How about this? If it's okay with your mom, why don't you come over tomorrow to watch football with me?"

Both of them look at me for permission. "We're going to carve pumpkins in the morning with Kate, but you can go after that. The games won't be on until the afternoon anyway."

I sigh at the total cuteness of the two of them as their wide-eyed, hopeful expressions turn to smiles of joy.

"That sounds perfect. How about I pick you up just before noon? That will give us time to grab a pizza and get back here before kick-off."

They're still both watching me for approval.

"That works."

Michael cheers. Dad holds out his hand for a high five. Michael quickly obliges. Hugs are given all around, and we head out. The exhaustion of the week is really catching up with me. If we leave now, I'll have just enough time to read Michael a bedtime story before falling into bed myself.

Chapter Eight

Will

Living next door to a beautiful woman has turned me into a stalker.

I haven't spoken with Melanie in a couple days, but I've seen her and Michael coming and going many times. I don't stand next to the window with binoculars or anything, but can I help it if I hear a car door slam and look out the window to see that she's leaving to take Michael to school? I probably could, but I don't want to.

From what I've seen this week, Melanie works on Mondays, Thursdays, and Fridays. Those are the days she wears nursing scrubs when she leaves in the morning. She and Michael head out around seven o'clock on those days, and they return at seven-thirty or later in the evening. Last night, it was eight-thirty when they got home. Again. Not exactly my fault that I happened to notice the time. I spend a lot of my days on the couch watching television, which is next to a window that has a view of Melanie's driveway.

Michael's voice gets my attention even now. A glance out the window from where I'm sitting allows me to see him bounding across the front yard toward Melanie's car. Melanie follows. No work today. She wears jeans and a light jacket to ward off the chill of this sunny October morning. She smiles as she unlocks the door of her Taurus, and she and Michael climb inside. Melanie sits in the driver's seat, turns on the car, and backs out of the driveway.

A heavy sigh escapes me. Why, I have no idea. I barely know the two of them, but I can't help wondering where they're off to at nine o'clock on a Saturday morning. Based solely on Michael's exuberance, it must be somewhere fun.

Aunt Bunny speaks very highly of Melanie. They've been neighbors for years now. Melanie checks on Bunny often, and Melanie was the one Bunny called when she fell. I know Melanie visited Bunny on Tuesday and on Thursday this week. It was the first thing Bunny said to me when I arrived for my visit on those days, and of course I got the talking-to yesterday. Does she give Melanie the same treatment when she visits?

The sound of a slamming car door breaks me from these thoughts. They're back already?

Nope. The silver BMW from the other day is parked in Melanie's driveway. The driver is headed to her front door.

Without a thought, I head out to greet him. By the time I get there, the man has made it to the front stoop.

"They're not home." Why I have to announce this, I have no idea. He'll figure that out on his own when Melanie doesn't answer the door.

He turns and looks at me. Melanie's ex is a decent looking guy, I suppose, with black hair and tanned skin as if he spends a lot of time out in the sun. If appearance is any way to judge, he doesn't look like he spent time in prison. He has no visible tattoos. He's clean shaven and carries a bouquet of flowers. When I reach him, he steps down the two steps to the walkway.

"Who're you?"

"I'm Will. I live next door."

"Bunny lives next door."

"She's my aunt. I live with her."

"So, go home. What do you have to do with Melanie?" He stares at me with eyes the color of steel. I stand straighter. I have a couple inches on this guy, and I could take him, but he's no slacker. Maybe he learned a few tricks while in the slammer, but I'm a Marine. I know a few tricks of my own.

Had Melanie really been married to this jerk? It

seems unbelievable, but at the same time, I don't really know her.

"That's none of your business. Who the hell are you?"

"Mel's husband."

"*Ex*-husband." Thank you, Aunt Bunny, for filling me in a little on Melanie's history.

"I won't be an *ex* for long, so stay the hell away from her and Michael."

"No chance. Melanie doesn't want you here and neither do I. You can leave now."

"I will, but only because Mel isn't here. I'll be back."

I clamp down every urge I have to punch this asshole and step out of his way so he can walk back to his car. He does. I stand in that same spot until I can no longer see his car.

"Whatcha doing?"

Michael's voice sounds so small. I turn to see him standing behind me. I didn't even hear him walk up. I thought it was crazy that Melanie didn't hear me approach that night she hit me, but here I am, being bested by a four-year-old. Of course, I was in my own world at the time.

"I'm cleaning the leaves out of Aunt Bunny's beds. That big tree has made a real mess of the front yard."

"It's an oak tree," Michael says shyly. He looks down at the ground and shuffles his right foot to the side. "We learned about them in school."

I prop the rake against the house and look towards Melanie's. It's hard to believe she let Michael come over here by himself. Unless...

"Does your mom know where you are?" He peeks up at me and then gives his head a shake. "Let's go find her and ask her if you can help me with all these leaves. Sound good?"

Michael's face brightens. We walk only a few steps toward their house before Melanie comes running around from their back yard. Her eyes, wide with worry, instantly tear up as she sees us. Two women follow close behind. I can feel their sighs of relief as Melanie kneels down and brings Michael in for a hug. Her eyes close as she holds him tightly.

"We were just coming to find you."

Melanie stands and wraps her arms around me just as tightly as she was holding Michael.

Um.

This was unexpected.

I tentatively bring my arms up to return her embrace loosely. Melanie smells really good, something floral mixed with the outdoors. I could hear them in the back yard, and in an effort to curb my stalker tendencies, I've made sure to stay firmly planted out front where I can't spy on them.

My gaze meets that of the younger of Melanie's friends. Her lips curve inward in an effort to not smile. The older woman isn't trying not to smile. She's beaming from ear to ear. I don't know how to react since this embrace has gone on longer than a friendly, thank-you hug. Melanie must realize this as well because she jumps back out of my arms as if she's just been shocked into movement. Her face is now a rosy red—whether from embarrassment or anger or both, I'm not sure. Michael looks from his mom to me. A huge grin spreads across his face.

"You wipe that smile off your face, young man." He does. Michael's smile disappears instantly as he turns to face Melanie. Her hands move to her hips. I brace myself for what's coming next.

"Will." Melanie speaks my name sharply, definitely not what I was expecting. I thought she was going to yell at Michael. She clears her throat. "This is my friend, Kate Simms, and her mother, Grace Richardson." Her words begin short and tempered but soften by the end of the sentence. Introductions. She's introducing me to her friends.

"It's nice to meet you, ladies." I step forward and shake each of their hands in turn. Kate's a redhead with fair skin and freckles. She's very pretty, but nothing like Melanie. *Where did that thought come from?* Since when do I compare women to Melanie?

I turn to Grace, who has short gray—almost silver—hair, light blue eyes, and a roundish face and body that appear only rounder with the oversized, bright orange sweater with a jack-o-lantern embellished on the front. "You're wearing the perfect sweater for pumpkin carving."

"Why thank you. I like to get into the spirit of things."

She somehow oozes mom-ness. Is that a thing? I like her immediately.

Melanie speaks again and draws me out of my warm thoughts of homemade cookies.

"Why did you walk away like that?"

Poor little Michael's eyes fill with tears. "I'm sorry, Mommy. I finished my pumpkin, and I heard a noise over here, so I wanted to see what it was. Will said I can help him rake leaves. Can I, Mom?"

Melanie's angry-mom eyes turn to me. I feel the heat of them along with the looks of the others in the group.

"There are a lot of leaves there. Would it be okay if Michael helped me out for a little while?"

Melanie studies me a bit longer, her anger abating slowly.

"Are you sure he won't be any trouble?"

"Absolutely not." Michael's grin is back and bigger than ever. "You ladies go ahead and carve your pumpkins. We men have work to do." Melanie bites her lower lip. "Please don't worry. We'll stay right here, and I promise to keep a close eye on him."

Melanie kneels down next to Michael. The sunlight hits Melanie's long, brown hair in a way that makes it shine even more. "Do you promise to stay with Will and not run off?"

"Yes, Mommy."

"Okay, you two have fun."

Michael squeals. "Thank you." Melanie mouths the words more than saying them out loud. Somehow that makes me feel warm inside.

Chapter Nine

Melanie

"Should I be worried about the fact that Michael is being watched by a man who's practically a stranger?"

"He sure didn't look like a stranger, the way you latched onto him like that." Kate puts a fresh cup of hot apple cider down on the table in front of me. "Besides, he's Bunny's nephew, they're right out front, and he's totally hot."

That hug.

So embarrassing. I clear my throat.

"Yeah. I don't know what that was. I was just so relieved to find Michael; I wasn't thinking straight."

"I'd say your thinking is fine. In fact, you should

do that a hell of a lot more often." Grace beams.

The tell-tale heat of a blush travels up my neck into my cheeks. Seriously. *What was I thinking with that move?* I wasn't thinking...at all. I found Michael. He was safe with Will, who was bringing him to find me. All this motherly emotion swirled inside of me, and I was so relieved.

Kate, Grace, and I are back on my patio to continue our pumpkin carving. I've been waiting for Kate to mention Grace's cancer, but she hasn't said a word. I'll keep my mouth shut, of course, but I don't like withholding information from my best friend.

It's not right. Grace should tell her children. This is cancer. What I said to Grace earlier this week is true; she can come out of this as healthy as ever. But, she needs to move ahead with treatment, and she needs her loved ones around her for support. As if she can tell what I'm thinking, she looks at me apologetically and gives a quick shrug of her shoulders.

This whole pumpkin-carving activity was Kate's idea. She's documenting the experience for her blog. She has a home decorating blog that she still runs, even though she's now married and running her family's store. She has part of her blog logo—a floor lamp with a tilted shade—carved into her extra-large pumpkin. So far, Kate's spent most of her time here taking photos of the rest of us, especially Michael, and making sure we have a fresh supply of hot apple cider and kettle corn. She's so good at entertaining, and she's one of those people who seem to do everything just right. She can't seem to help herself. Just like she and Grace can't help themselves from pairing me up with my handsome neighbor.

"I don't think that's going to happen, Grace, but thanks for your suggestion." *Not.*

"Why not, sweetie? Will's handsome and caring. You were worried about Michael, but you should have seen how worried Will was about you. It was written all over his face, and when you hugged him, he looked very happy with the situation."

Big sigh. Why am I reluctant to get to know Will better?

"Well, to start with, he's going through something. I don't know what it is, but I think he's here for reasons other than taking care of Bunny's house. We didn't get off to the best start. I assaulted him while I was trespassing in his—well, Bunny's— yard. He slammed the door in my face when I made him apology muffins, and he won't be in town permanently. I don't want to get wrapped up in any kind of relationship with someone I know is leaving. That isn't good for me or for Michael, who's obviously in love with Will already."

Kate plops down in the chair next to me. "Those are impediments, possibly. The *assault*, as you put it, and the door-slamming incident are in the past. That much was obvious after your embrace in the front yard a few minutes ago. The part that could be a problem is why he's here and how long he plans to stay in town. You should ask him. Or, better yet, ask Bunny."

Grace nods. "Knowing Bunny, I'm surprised she hasn't been meddling in your business, trying to get the two of you hooked up. She's like that."

"She's not the only one," I say with a chuckle. Grace smiles. It's easy to talk honestly with these two without them taking offense. "There's another big reason as well." They both look at me expectantly. Don't they know? "Malcolm."

"Malcolm?" Kate scoffs. "What does he have to do with anything?"

"I don't want him to cause any trouble. He already saw Will with me last week. If Malcolm thinks something is going on, he might use it against me."

"That's ridiculous. Malcolm no longer has a place in your life or Michael's, for that matter. He'll figure that out—soon hopefully—and go away. You have signed divorce papers where he relinquished parental rights."

"I guess."

Grace chimes in now. "Malcolm is an asshole father who bailed on his pregnant wife and unborn son. He can forget any further claim to Michael."

I gnaw on my lower lip, something I tend to do when I'm nervous. I sure wish my own mother had Grace's attitude. Grace would never ask me to consider taking Malcolm back. She leans back in her chair and waits for my response, studying me with caring eyes.

"I hope that's true."

"Of course it is. Malcolm will get bored. Hopefully sooner rather than later."

"Are you sure you won't reconsider your plans for tonight?"

We're cleaning up the pumpkin guts and other mess we made on my patio table. Of course, clean-up is easy, thanks to Kate having brought a disposable plastic tablecloth. We fold it all up together and toss the ball into a big black garbage bag.

"I'm looking forward to a relaxing evening with Michael. Maybe we'll snuggle on the couch and watch a Disney movie. That's about all I can manage right now. I certainly can't take a night at bingo with Granny Simms."

Kate and Hunter have standing plans to take Hunter's granny to bingo every Saturday night. The problem with tonight is that Hunter has to work.

"I don't know if I can handle Granny by myself."

The thought of Kate actually handling Granny makes me laugh out loud. "Granny's calmer now that she's dating Frank and much less likely to get into trouble. You'll be fine on your own."

"Not in my current condition." The corners of Kate's mouth curve up into a grin. What the heck does that mean? I look at Grace for a clue. Her head is tilted, her eyebrows raised.

That's why Grace hasn't told Kate her news yet. Kate has news of her own, and it's the happiest kind.

"Oh my gosh, Kate, are you pregnant?"

The wattage of Kate's smile turns to blinding. My eyes are instantly full of tears. I scream, at least I think it was me. There's suddenly a lot of noise from the three of us as I hug Kate, and Grace hugs her, too, although I can tell she already knew. This is so exciting. Kate and Hunter were married this past June and are already starting their family.

"You said you wanted to have children right away. You sure weren't kidding. What did Hunter say?"

"He's so happy. He wants a girl. Isn't that great? Big, macho Hunter wants a daughter. Makes me love him even more, if that's possible."

I force the pang of jealousy away. Unlike Malcolm, I bet Hunter had been excited to learn that he's going to be a father. I bet Kate told him right away, and they danced around the bathroom together.

"The baby's due next June. I'm finally going to be a grandma." Grace smiles, her eyes wet with tears. This will likely be the most spoiled child in the entire state of Virginia.

"June twenty-first, to be exact. It seems like an eternity."

"It'll be here before you know it."

"All right, I've only told Dad and the two of you. I have to tell Brady as soon as possible, before his feelings get hurt."

I lift Kate's pumpkin for her and carry it around the house to her CRV. "This thing weighs a ton. You should have asked for my help carrying it when you got here. You have to think of the baby, you know."

"It weighed less than twenty pounds, and that was before we gutted it. I'm fine. I don't want to be babied."

"Hi, Mommy!" Michael shouts from next door. I look over to see that he and Will have raked the leaves into one enormous pile. Michael stands right in the middle of it with a giant smile on his face. I give him a wave. Both Michael and Will wave back. Will isn't in the pile, but his smile is as big, or possibly even bigger, than Michael's. Letting Michael go with Will was the right thing to do.

"It's okay if you tell Michael about the baby. He'll be happy, won't he?"

I hug Kate to me. "He'll be thrilled."

We say our goodbyes, and I head across the yard to check on their progress.

"Everything okay?" Will asks first thing. "It looked like there was an awful lot of hugging going on over there, or do you and Kate always have such tearful goodbyes?"

I smile. "Today was special. Kate just told us that she's pregnant."

Will's eyes widen slightly at the news. Michael pops out of the leaves and runs to my side.

"Aunt Kate's going to have a baby?" Michael looks at me with such joy in his expression.

I nod. He screams happily and runs through the middle of the pile, scattering leaves all around.

"I'm sorry, he's making such a mess of your leaves."

Will chuckles. "Michael helped rake these leaves. He knows what he has to do now." Sure enough, Michael circles back toward us, grabs a rake, and begins working feverishly, laughing the whole time.

"Mommy, it's the most fun to fall backwards into the leaves. Will and I have done it lots of times. You have to do it, too."

"Okay. I'll give it a try." Michael continues working. I turn to Will and stand as tall as I can and swallow. "I'm sorry about earlier." Will's forehead furrows. "About um, latching onto you like that. I don't know what came over me. I'm sorry."

"There's no need to apologize."

Will squeezes my forearm in what's surely meant to be a comforting gesture. It's anything but. Heat and electricity emanate from that spot and pulse through my body. I step back, breaking the connection. Did Will feel that, too? The way he stares at his hand tells me he felt something. We're saved from further embarrassment by Michael, thank goodness.

"Ready?" He runs to me, takes my hand, and pulls me to the edge of the leaf pile. He continues to hold my hand as he waits for Will to join us. Will, who seems to be familiar with the routine, takes Michael's other hand.

"We count to three and then fall backwards. Don't worry, Mommy, it won't hurt." I return his smile. His eyes and then his whole face shine with excitement. He's beautiful. "Okay. Ready?"

"Ready," Will and I both say in unison.

We count together. "One. Two. Three."

Whoosh. We fall backward together, and honestly, it really is fun. I haven't done this in years, but the memories flow through my mind like it was only a few months ago. The smell of the leaves all around me brings back a memory of Kate and me hiding in a leaf pile when we played hide and seek with her brother, Brady, at their family cabin. We played in that pile of leaves all afternoon that day.

I sit up and see Will sitting across from me, smiling from ear to ear. Dry leaves hang from his sweater. I look down and see they're attached to mine as well. He reaches toward me and removes a leaf from my hair. I can't help but smile.

"Where's Michael?" a little voice asks from somewhere in the void between us.

"Where is Michael?" I answer back, faux concern in my voice.

"I don't know," Will answers, playing along. "Is he

here?"

He curls his hand and wiggles his fingers before submerging it into the leaves. Shrieks of happiness cut through the quiet until he removes his hand from the leaves.

I continue the charade. "Maybe he's over here." My tickling fingers connect with Michael's side as he erupts in laughter. Michael sits up quickly, the two of us narrowly missing a collision of heads. I pull back as he throws his hands up into the air and showers us all with leaves.

Will laughs a deep belly laugh and launches into tickling Michael. Michael rolls around in the leaves, laughing and loving every second of this time. A warmth begins to fill me as I watch them play together. Michael's missing out on this type of male companionship. He has my dad, but that isn't the same. Speaking of dad, it's about time for their football date. I remember just as I hear the sound of a car pulling into our driveway.

It's not Dad's car.

It's Malcolm. He pulls his BMW right into my driveway.

Good feeling gone.

Will makes eye contact with me, and his smile immediately fades. I turn back to see Malcolm standing next to his car, flowers in hand, watching us.

"Who's that?"

My eyes take in Michael's curious expression. He

can't know who Malcolm really is.

"That's a friend of mine from work."

I manage to choke out the words. They sound completely fake to my ears and must to Michael's as well because he turns toward me as if to gauge their truthfulness. I take a deep breath and force myself to look calm on the outside—if that's even possible. My insides feel like they're vibrating.

"Since we worked so hard on these leaves, why don't we grab some lemonade and a couple of the chocolate chip cookies I bought yesterday at the grocery store?"

"Would that be okay, Mommy?"

"Sure, sweetie. You've earned them after all your hard work, which you'll have to do again after the mess we just made." I add a laugh at the end. So. Fake.

Fortunately, Will doesn't give Michael time to figure that out. He stands, brushes off the leaves with a couple big swipes, and extends his hand to Michael. Michael takes it, and the two of them walk together into Bunny's house. Michael doesn't look back, but Will does just before closing the door behind them.

With a heavy sigh, I stand and walk across the yard to where Malcolm is waiting next to his car.

He's shaved today, and he's dressed up, too. He wears khakis and a dark green golf shirt. Both items are still creased from their packaging. He doesn't need to step up his game. It's too late now for any effort.

I hug my arms to me. There's no point in being nice to him, so I get right to the point.

"Why are you here?" Malcolm sends me a small, apologetic smile. I saw this smile a lot in those few months that we were together. This move used to work for him. Now, I'm immune. "Well?"

His smile fades. He holds a bouquet of flowers toward me. I keep my arms crossed and don't take them. He sighs and sets the flowers on top of his car.

"I told you the other day. I was an idiot when we were together. It felt like everything was happening so fast. I wasn't used to being married yet. I couldn't handle a baby on top of that."

"That's not what you said when you served me with the divorce papers. I believe you blamed me for messing up your life."

"I was a fool then."

"And you think you're better now?"

"I am. Your mother can see it." My eyes roll seemingly on their own. "She agrees that we should at least give it a try. You loved me once. Maybe you can love me again."

"I did love you, but that was a long time ago. I'm very much over you."

"Think you're moving on with that guy?"

I know he means Will, but I ask him anyway. "What guy?"

He nods his head toward Bunny's house. "He's not the man you need."

"And you are?" I don't give him a chance to answer. "You need to leave immediately and don't come back. You made it clear that you never wanted to see me or Michael again, and now you get to stick with that decision. You stay away from Michael, you stay away from me, and you stay away from my family. Do you understand?"

Malcolm's expression is the epitome of remorse. "I understand it might take some time to get used to the idea but try. I still love you, Mel. I could move back in the house with you and Michael. We could be a family."

"No chance. Michael is *my* son, and this is *my* house."

Malcolm takes a step toward me, but he must think better of it because he moves no closer. He studies me with his soft, blue eyes. A chill runs through me, causing the hairs on my arms to stick up—clearly not the reaction he seems to be hoping for. He's wasting his time. I'll never go back with him, and there's no way in hell he's ever stepping foot into my home.

In a stroke of good luck, Dad picks this moment to pull into the driveway. He pulls his Audi up close to us and next to Malcolm's car. I know before he even gets out of the car that he's unhappy about seeing Malcolm here.

"Malcolm, it's pretty clear from the look on Melanie's face that she doesn't want you here."

Malcolm looks down at his feet as he shifts them

from side to side. "I was just taking this opportunity to tell Mel all the things I spoke with you and Patricia about yesterday. She needs to understand how I feel. I love her."

Malcolm looks up and speaks the last words directly to me. He's using his apology eyes again. Visions of past moments when he used these eyes on me flow through my mind.

I'm done.

"That really seems to be the way you work."

"What?"

"You do whatever you want and then apologize for it later. What is it you used to say? It's easier to ask for forgiveness than permission? I can't forgive you for walking out on your son. Now, I've heard what you came to say. I want you to leave. Stay away from us."

"It's one thing if you don't want me back, but I'm that boy's father. I deserve to be in his life."

"You gave up your rights to Michael, and you've never paid a dime of child support. You deserve nothing."

"We bought this house together, remember that?"

Only too well, but we only lived in this house together for five months. Since Malcolm left, I've done everything I can to erase any memory of him.

"Another thing you wanted no part of. I bought out your half of the house as part of the divorce settlement—at least the tiny bit of equity we had in it at the time. This house is mine, and you are not welcome on my property. Please leave."

Malcolm's eyes are far from apologetic now. He's seething, and his anger comes through loud and clear. He turns and picks up the bouquet of flowers from the roof of his car. He throws them on the ground before plopping into his car. Without another look at me or Dad, he starts the engine and backs out of the driveway. I don't know if he drives over the flowers on purpose or if it just happened that way, but the fragile roses are smashed into the pavement.

Dad's arm moves around my shoulders to console me. The funny thing is, I don't really feel like I need consoling. The feelings of rejection, loss, and anger I felt for so long don't surface. The anger is still here, but it's taken a different form. Instead of being angry with Malcolm for leaving Michael, I'm angry that he's returned. He made his choice, and now I just want him to go away.

Chapter Ten

Will

"Papa!" Michael shouts with excitement, and before I can stop him, he runs out my front door. Melanie's going to kill me. Or, maybe not. Her ex-husband is gone. Another man is here now, an older man, with his arm around her shoulders. He's tall with brown hair and a thin face. He looks a lot like Michael and enough like Melanie to know he has to be her father. He releases Melanie just in time to catch Michael as he jumps into his arms.

"Ready to go to lunch? Can we get chicken nuggets or pizza? Let's get pizza."

The gentleman smiles and lowers Michael to the ground. "Shhh. Don't talk about our lunch choices in front of your mom. That's a discussion we have in the car where she can't hear us."

Melanie smiles at his comment and then turns and directs it at me. Damn, if just the sight of her happy smile doesn't warm my insides. I need to nip these feelings right away, but for now, my priority is to make sure Melanie's okay.

"Dad, this is Will, Bunny's great-nephew. Will, this is my father, John."

John shakes my hand firmly. He eyes me up and down as he's likely done with many potential suitors. There's no need to go to the trouble since I am most definitely not one of Melanie's boyfriends. That doesn't stop me from wishing I could be.

"It's nice to meet you, John."

"So, you in town visiting Bunny?"

"Yes, sir. I have some time off, so I thought I might be more useful here than hanging around at home." And I needed some alone time. Mom and Dad have been smothering me since I've been home on leave.

"Will is a Marine. He was in Iraq."

"Really?" Just those few words, and John's whole attitude towards me changes. He stands a bit straighter. "Thank you for your service."

"Thank you, sir."

"Did you get to carry a gun?"

Michael looks up at me, his eyes the size of saucers.

"Sometimes. Guns are very dangerous, though.

You know that, right?"

"Oh, I know. Grayson Riley's dad takes him hunting sometimes. He got to hold the gun once, but he didn't get to shoot it. His dad says he has to be older before he gets to shoot it."

"He does."

"Are you ready to go, Michael?"

Michael gives Melanie a tight hug. "You be a good boy."

"Yes, Mommy."

Without another word, Michael opens the back door of the car, climbs into the back seat, and buckles himself into the car seat that's already there.

"We're outta here," John says with a chuckle. "Nice to meet you, Will. Mel, sweetie, I'll bring him home after the game." He looks from Melanie to me and then back to Melanie. "Enjoy your free afternoon. Do something fun."

Is that a hint for me to ask Melanie to do something? I can't do that.

Melanie's father gets into his car, and with a nod of his head, he backs out of the driveway, leaving Melanie and me alone.

Awkwardly alone.

I steal a glance toward Melanie and find her looking at me.

"Thank you for taking Michael inside when you did. I'm sorry you had to witness that. He's my ex-husband and is no longer a part of our lives." She sighs heavily. "Michael doesn't know him, and I want to keep it that way."

"I understand." Mostly because Aunt Bunny filled me in on some of the particulars. Like the fact that the bastard left Melanie when she was pregnant with Michael. "There's something you should know, though." Melanie's body instantly stiffens. "I don't think it's a big deal, considering how he was just here and all, but he did come by this morning while you were out."

Her expression is full of concern. "Did you talk to him?"

"I did. I recognized him as the guy who did the drive by last week. I didn't like him hanging around your house when you weren't home. I pretty much told him that, and he left."

"What did he say?"

"He told me who he was and that he was here to get you back." She nods. "Are those the flowers that he brought?"

An array of colorful and flattened petals lay in Melanie's driveway.

"Yeah. He ran over them when he left. That's a fitting end for flowers from Malcolm."

I scoop them up by the stems. Many petals fall to the ground, but most amazingly stay intact. "I'll get rid of these for you." I give her a small smile. "Enjoy your afternoon."

With just those few words, I walk back home to Bunny's.

I'm a chicken.

An hour later, I've successfully raked and bagged all the leaves in Bunny's front yard. Today is so much different than last Saturday. It was last Saturday that Melanie came over to apologize, and I shut the door in her face. I didn't slam it, not that it matters. Of course, that was only because slamming it would have hurt my aching head even more.

Melanie's chosen to spend her free afternoon sitting on her back patio. I can see her out the kitchen window. She's curled up under a blanket, reading a book. Maybe she's hungry, too. I came in here to find something for lunch. Maybe I can find something for both of us.

The thought pops into my head. It isn't the smartest idea, but I also know I'm going to do it anyway, so I begin the preparations. When everything's ready, I carry the tray over to Melanie's.

"What's all this?"

Her tone is tentative, but she smiles at me when she speaks. She turns her open book upside down and places it carefully on the side table next to her lounge chair so as not to lose her place.

"I promise not to bother you for long. This is just a little something I whipped up for you to nibble on while you're out here." I set the tray on the outdoor dining table and show her the bottle of Chardonnay. "Would you like a glass?"

Her tentative smile grows bigger. "I'd love one."

The bottle opens easily with a twist. I pour some into the wine glass as Melanie joins me at the table.

"You didn't have to get up."

"Where's your glass? You're not having any wine?"

"I don't want to take away from your alone time. I'm guessing you don't get much of it." She looks over the plate of cheese, crackers, and grapes I brought for her to enjoy with the wine.

"That's true, but I'd really like it if you'd stay and eat with me."

"Really?" While I was hoping for an invitation to join her, I don't know if I should accept.

"Yes. I'll get you a glass. Be right back."

She disappears into her house and returns quickly with another wine glass. I pour myself some, and we sit down together at the table.

"Thank you for this. It was really thoughtful."

"You're very welcome. It's the least I could do after the rough start we had." She smiles into her wine glass as she takes a long sip. The sun is high above us now. Its shine reflects off Melanie's chestnut hair in a glow. The warmth is back in my belly. I take my own sip of wine and feel even warmer. Time for a subject change. "Michael is a really great kid. Thanks for letting him come over to play."

She chuckles now, a soft sound that seems to hang in the air even after it's over. "He really is great, isn't he? I mean, I realize I'm very partial, but I think

Michael's amazing."

"He is amazing and smart, too. He knew what kind of leaves we were raking, and he likes me, so he's obviously brilliant."

"Obviously."

Melanie's eyes sparkle when she speaks of her son, so I keep the conversation moving in that direction.

"How old is Michael? Is he in kindergarten?"

"He'll be five next Saturday. He's a smart kid, but he missed the cut-off to start school this year, so he's in preschool for one more year. It's a good school though, and they keep him learning at his own pace. He's starting to read. That's really exciting for him. He loves books. He can't seem to get enough of them."

"You must be really proud. I'm sure it's difficult raising him on your own, but you're a great mom."

The words spill out before I can stop them. I didn't intend to bring any negativity into our conversation. I meant it strictly as a compliment because she really is an amazing mother. Melanie tugs on her lower lip—a reaction that makes me want to kiss away any stress that caused the gesture in the first place. She looks away from me and focuses on something across the yard. She hugs her wine glass to her chest and absentmindedly moves her index finger back and forth around the base of the glass.

"I have a lot of help. My parents watch Michael

when I'm working. For years I worked the evening shift at the hospital. Things are easier now that I work during the day and Michael's in preschool." I nod my understanding. That must have been really difficult at times. "I haven't taken money from them though, although they've certainly offered it enough. I'm thankful for their offers in case I ever need it, but we've done okay so far. I do okay at the hospital, and my Aunt Maggie passed away a couple years ago. She wasn't rich or anything, but she left the proceeds from her house to a trust fund for Michael. His college is paid for, so that's one less thing to worry about."

Melanie blushes slightly as if she went a little more personal that she intended. A moment of silence passes, and I change the subject altogether.

"Kate seems like a good friend."

Her gaze moves back to me. "She's the best. I've known her since kindergarten. We've been through a lot together."

"Geez. I haven't known anyone that long. My father was also a Marine, so we moved around a lot when I was a kid. I had friends, but I never stayed in touch with any of them long-term. I met my best friend during my senior year of high school. We joined the Marines together."

"Do you get to see him often?"

"Not really, although he's planning to visit in a couple weeks." We'll see if that pans out, though. Alex is reliable. I think it's just that I don't want to get my hopes up and then have him not show up.

"Why are you here, really?" Melanie's question takes me completely by surprise, although it shouldn't. "You didn't need to come here to take care of Bunny's house. So, why did you come?"

"Bunny didn't tell you?" She gives her head a slight shake. "That's surprising. Bunny doesn't have many secrets."

Melanie smiles. "So, why?"

"Aunt Bunny thought I needed a change of scenery."

She nods thoughtfully. "She told me you were injured in Iraq and on medical leave while you recuperate. She said you saved a little boy during a raid, and you were given a medal for your bravery." I shrug. All true, but it sounds so much better when Melanie says it like that. Living it is so much different. "Will you tell me about it?"

Will I? Geez. I've barely talked about it with anyone outside of my command. But, there's something different about today, about being with Melanie here like this, that makes me think it'll be okay to tell her. I look into those beautiful brown eyes of hers, so soft and caring, and the decision is made.

"We were on a special mission near Tikrit, working with the Iraqi military. Things had been fairly calm—for that part of the world anyway. A few of us were with some Iraqi soldiers on patrol. There were plenty of people milling around on their way to and from the market. That's when it happened. Machine gun fire sent everyone scrambling. A woman who'd been walking with her son was hit. She fell to the sand-covered road. Her son knelt down beside her. I called to him, but he wouldn't come to me."

I pause and close my eyes until the intense memories pass: the heat of that day, the smell of the spices from the market, the pop of the gunfire, and what haunts me more than anything, the dark eyes of the boy.

"Do you want to take a break?"

Melanie.

My eyelids flutter open to a completely different view. Caring brown eyes look back at me. I take a deep breath and let the coolness of the fall air seep into my lungs and my consciousness. I'm far away from Tikrit, yet I feel connected with the area somehow, as if pulled by an invisible tether that can't be broken.

"I want to finish."

She leans closer and intertwines her fingers with mine. I can't remember the last time I held hands with a woman. It gives me the strength I need to get through the rest of my story.

"The shots were coming from the second story of a building on a corner just ahead of us. We were shooting back and took cover behind a produce cart someone had left in the street. The boy—Kasim— was kneeling in the middle of the street. He wouldn't move away from his mother. She was likely dead or unconscious at best. Either way, I didn't think she was going to make it. An explosive round fell into the street. I didn't think. I just launched myself and covered the boy's body and his mother's as best I could."

Melanie brings her other hand to our clasped ones and grips tightly. Tears slide down her cheeks.

"And the boy lived." She speaks the words quietly.

"He did. His mother did too, somehow. She was shot in the back. Turns out they were the family of a wealthy man in town. The woman was taken to the hospital, had surgery, and made it through. Kasim only had a couple bruises."

"And you?"

"The blast knocked me unconscious. I woke up in the military hospital on base. I couldn't believe that we'd gotten out of there alive. Reinforcements came to aid us right after the blast, and the threat was eliminated."

"You were so brave. You saved Kasim and his mother."

Melanie's full-on crying now. I gently wipe the tears from her cheeks, but they're immediately replaced by more.

"Everyone says that. I did what anyone would have done in that situation. I did my job."

She shakes her head but doesn't argue. "What injuries did you have from the blast?"

"Only a concussion. The soldiers who were with

me say it was a miracle I survived at all."

"But you did survive."

I shrug. "I guess, but what I'm doing now doesn't feel like surviving. It sucks."

"Bunny worried about you a lot when you were over there." I breathe out a heavy sigh, but instead of relieving the pressure, my lungs feel even more weighed down. I know she did. She sent me a lot of letters. "When you came back to the states, you went to your family in Florida?"

"Yeah." It seems like Melanie wants more here, but I don't know what she's looking for.

"You were with your family down there to help you recover, so why did you leave them and come up here to Virginia to sit alone in Bunny's house all day? That's the part I don't understand."

Right to the point, I guess. I don't know the answers exactly myself, but I do my best.

"My parents are wonderful and caring people—they really are. I just began to feel suffocated. My injuries now aren't physical. It's all in here." I point to my head. "I can't seem to get past what happened that day."

"You have PTSD." It's a statement, not a question, but I confirm with a nod anyway. Melanie's thoughtful for a few moments and then asks, "You have headaches?" I nod again. "And nightmares?"

"Killer nightmares where I relive parts of that day over and over. The nightmares were getting worse, so when Aunt Bunny invited me here, I accepted. I was hoping a change of scenery might help. That's why I came here."

"Is it working? Are they any better?"

"No, but they're not any worse, either. Sometimes I get physical in my sleep. Two nights ago, I broke the lamp Aunt Bunny had on the nightstand in the room where I'm sleeping. I haven't told her yet."

"She'll understand."

"I know she will, but I don't know how to get past this. I feel broken."

"Are you seeing someone to help you with all of this?"

"I had been back at home. I have an appointment at the VA hospital in Salem on Tuesday."

"I'll go with you."

"You don't have to do that."

"I'm a nurse, Will. And a friend. Let me help you."

A friend. I could really use one of those right now.

"I'd really like that. Thank you."

Melanie smiles, and the warmth returns to my stomach. This woman is amazing.

Chapter Eleven

Melanie

My tears are finally beginning to subside. I've seen a lot of pain in my life, but the horror Will's eyes just displayed are a rare sight, even for an ER nurse. I sit up straighter in my chair and realize I'm still holding on to Will's hand with all my might. While it likely appears on the outside that I am holding Will's hand to console him, I need comforting as well.

I look down at our entwined fingers. His hands are strong. His body is strong...strong enough to protect that little boy and his mother from the blast. Will could have died. Shoot, he probably should have died, but he hadn't. He's somehow here with me now to bring me cheese and crackers and sit here with me on my patio, where I've never sat alone with a man other than Malcolm.

If one of a thousand things had changed that day in Tikrit, Will wouldn't be here with me right now. The tears start again, and this time, they're more than a few stray tears. They come in sobs. So much emotion wells up inside of me for a man that I've known only a week, and yet, somehow I feel like I've known him much longer.

Will's strong arms move around me and pull me to him. When that isn't as comfortable as it should be, he stands and tugs me up with him. My arms move around his waist. My head rests against his chest. *Much better.* I breathe in the smell of fall from the dried leaves he spent the morning raking. A tightness forms in the pit of my stomach. If it feels this good to be held in his arms, what would it feel like to kiss his lips?

He leans back enough so our eyes can meet. They're darker than I've ever seen them. A wave of dizziness travels over me. But, it feels good—nerves mixed with the hope that Will might kiss me.

"It kills me when you do that," he says, his words softly spoken, barely a whisper.

"What?"

"Bite your lower lip. It's sexy as hell, but it means you're anxious about something. Are you afraid I'm going to kiss you?"

"I'm afraid you're *not* going to kiss me."

Will's eyes darken even more, but that's all I see before I close my own and feel his lips on mine. Soft, so soft and unsure. A tingling moves through me and then a shiver. He pulls me closer again as our kiss deepens. A moan releases from somewhere deep inside me. Instead of moving things even further, it's as if the sound scares him somehow.

He pulls away. His eyes are no longer dark with need. Now, Will's the one who's worried. I don't want that look in his eyes. I want him to want me. He twists a piece of my hair around his finger.

"I wish I'd met you and Michael *before*. I'm in a hole right now, and I'm not going to drag you into it with me. I can't let that happen."

"Will you let me be your friend?"

He nods softly. "I never meant to take up so much of your alone time. I'll see you later, okay?"

My turn to nod. He kisses me lightly on the cheek and walks back to Bunny's house.

Three hours later, and my knees are still weak from Will's kiss. That's never happened before. Not when Malcolm kissed me, or anyone else for that matter. I snuggle back into the lounge chair and sigh. It's more than just the kiss. Will had said, *"I wish I'd met you and Michael before."* He cares about Michael. Even if Will hadn't said the words, it's obvious he cares about my son. The way they played together with the leaves is a sure indication.

Do Will and I have a chance for any kind of future together? Sure, it isn't a good time for Will to be in a relationship, but I can still be there for him. I can help him get through this. Besides, maybe he needs me.

Geez. That does sound like me. Am I really attracted to Will, or am I only sensing that he needs help, and I'm happy to be his Florence Nightingale? That's what Mom always says. I try to take care of everyone. That was what attracted me to Malcolm in the beginning. He'd looked so pitiful when he'd come into the ER. It's not like a sprained ankle is anything serious, but that was the catalyst to get me talking to him. After that, I was sucked in by his charms and married him just a couple months later. That was such a stupid move.

Is that what I'm doing here? Am I pulled to Will because of his PTSD? If that were the case, then I wouldn't be so affected by his kiss. It was the shortest kiss of all time, and yet it affected me more than any other kiss I've ever had.

And the way the corners of Will's eyes scrunch up when he smiles. I haven't seen many of them, but he was smiling when he was playing in the leaves with Michael. He was happy for a short time out there. We all were.

While I do need to proceed with caution, there's nothing wrong with being Will's friend—he certainly could use one—and then seeing where that leads. The last thing I need to do is jump into a relationship with anyone. I learned from my experience with Malcolm that I need to take things very slowly before I commit to anyone. Will certainly needs to focus on other things. This works.

"Mommy!" Michael runs to me and hops next to my chair, bubbling over with excitement. "Virginia won. We cheered for them, and they won."

A laugh escapes me. Dad walks around the house from the front yard wearing a huge smile. "Well, you and Papa did a good job then."

I stand and bring Michael in for a hug.

"It was a nail-biter. Hail Mary pass in the last few seconds to score the winning touchdown. *Phew*. It was a tough one. Michael did a great job of understanding the game."

"Can I play football, Mommy?"

"It's too late to play this year. It's almost time for basketball though. Would you like to try that?" *Please try basketball or soccer or some other sport where concussions aren't as prevalent as football.*

"Can we watch basketball, Papa?"

"Sure we can. Next time you come over, we'll learn about basketball."

Michael smiles and heads into the house.

"Thanks, Dad, for taking Michael this afternoon. He's obviously thrilled."

"We had a great time. He's such a good boy. You've done a good job with him, Mel."

"I couldn't have done it without you and Mom.

You have to take some credit too."

Dad shifts his weight and looks down at the patio and then back at me. "Everything okay here after I left? Did Malcolm come back?"

"No."

"So that's from you and Will?" Dad nods toward the table and the half eaten cheese platter and two empty wine glasses.

"Will saw me sitting out here and brought all of that over. I will never sit and chat with Malcolm about anything."

Dad raises his eyebrows. "Will seems like a nice man."

"We're just friends."

For now.

Hopefully.

Dad nods his head with a small smile. "If you say so. You and Michael have a good night. I'll see you when you pick up Michael after work on Monday, if not sooner."

I give him a quick hug. "Bye, Dad."

"See you soon, sweetheart."

Dad walks back toward the front of the house. A shiver runs through me. The sun has dipped below the tops of the trees. Without its warmth, my patio is no longer warm. I place the wine glasses and bottle on the tray with the cheese platter and carry all of it into my kitchen and set it on the counter next to the sink. Michael joins me there, still smiling from his great afternoon.

"Mommy, can I go visit Will for a minute?"

A huge sigh escapes me. "Why do you want to see Will?"

"Raking leaves with him this morning was fun. I want to ask him if we can rake at our house tomorrow."

"I'm glad you had fun with Will, but we can't ask him to rake our leaves. You and I can spend some time raking tomorrow afternoon."

Michael's smile droops a bit. I don't blame him. I'd like to spend more time with Will myself.

"Can we invite Will to dinner tonight?"

Can we? I catch myself biting my lower lip. I do bite my lip when I'm anxious, just like Will said. *Before he kissed me.* The warmth of remembrance spreads through me. Maybe it'd be okay to invite Will over for dinner. There's no telling what he's eating over there by himself. We're having hamburgers and broccoli.

"Let me get these dishes cleaned up, and we can ask Will to dinner when I return them."

Michael's cheer is practically deafening. I feel the same way—at least, I will if Will accepts the invitation. I know I shouldn't get all worked up about a man who's told me he only wants a friend right now. I do want to be a good friend to Will, but after the kiss we shared, I'm not sure that's all he really wants from me. There's no way we could have a kiss like that and not take things further. Our kiss had an effect on Will as well. I could see it in his eyes. Maybe he's been over there all day thinking about me, like I've been here thinking about him.

I quickly wash and dry the platter and glasses. The glass that's mine goes back in the cabinet, and I place the rest of the dishes on the tray. Michael opens and closes the door for us as we head back outside and over to Bunny's house.

Michael chats the whole way about the possibility of playing basketball. I make a mental note to look into recreational leagues for kids his age.

Will answers the door right away and with a smile. He's happy to see us. No migraine this time. Thank goodness.

"Hi," I say quietly as I hand the tray to him. He takes it from me and places it on the small table Bunny has just to the left of her front door. "Thanks again for the wine and cheese. That was a really nice surprise." *As was the kiss we shared.* I keep that thought to myself, yet it feels somehow like Will knows my thoughts.

"Hi, Will," Michael says excitedly as if the words are bursting out of him. "Wanna come to our house for dinner tonight?"

Will's eyes find mine and study me as if to gauge my thoughts about this dinner invitation. I give him a small quick nod as a signal to show I'm good with it. But is Will good with it? He keeps Michael and me guessing for a couple long seconds. He looks back to Michael and furrows his forehead.

"I guess that depends." He looks at Michael directly. "What are you having for dinner tonight?"

Michael looks at me. "What are we having, Mommy?"

"Hamburgers and broccoli."

"Broccoli?" Will's eyes widen but not in horror. It sounds as if that's the best news he's heard all day. "That's my favorite. I wouldn't miss it. Thank you for inviting me."

Michael beams. My face feels hot. There's no telling what kind of message I'm giving off right now. I turn my attention to Michael.

"Okay, sweetie. Let's get going. We'll see Will soon."

Will shines some of his huge smile on me now. My tummy curls. I have it bad for this guy. I really do. I force a polite smile onto my face.

"We'll be ready to eat at six-thirty. You can come over any time."

"Thank you, Melanie."

Chapter Twelve

Will

Spending this much time with Melanie in one day can't be good for me. I mean, it's great for me. But it isn't good for Melanie. I can't allow myself to be this selfish. Sure, today is a good day, but what about tomorrow when I'm in the throes of depression? What about the next day when my head hurts so much I wish it would just explode and end the pain?

But right now, at this moment, it's hard to remember any of the bad things going on in my life. Melanie grilled cheeseburgers and steamed broccoli, and everything tasted delicious. Now, we're sitting close together on the couch with Michael in the middle, watching Duke play Virginia Tech. Michael's fascinated by the game of football and by the thought that I played during high school. I field question after question and promise to teach him to throw sometime soon.

It's just before nine o'clock when I realize Michael's down for the count. His little head has been resting against my arm for a while. When he doesn't react to an interception, I know something's up. It's as if Melanie and I both notice at the same time. Her eyes meet mine, and we share a knowing smile.

"Let me carry Michael to bed. I'll be right back." Melanie stands and looks down at us.

"Would it be okay if I do it?"

"Sure."

I lift my arm slowly until Michael rests against my side. This new position is much easier to reach underneath his back and legs and lift him up off the couch. He's light as a feather and completely zonked. Michael shows no sign of waking up.

"Right this way."

I follow Melanie up the stairs and then take a quick left turn into Michael's bedroom. The lamp beside his bed is lit, revealing his bedroom decorated in various shades of blue with lots of red firetrucks. Melanie pulls the covers to the side. I lay Michael carefully on his bed and watch as Melanie pulls the covers over him and kisses him lightly on the forehead. She turns off the lamp, and we retrace our steps down the stairs to the living room.

What happens next?

"You don't have to leave, you know. Why don't you stay and watch the rest of the game?"

I shouldn't stay—I know that—but the thought of being alone at Aunt Bunny's when I could be here with Melanie leaves me cold. Of course I'm staying.

"Thanks. I'd like that."

We share a smile and reclaim our seats on the sofa, keeping the space between us empty where Michael had sat.

"Thank you for entertaining all of Michael's football questions. It's good that you were here. I didn't know the answers to half of them."

"You don't want him to play, do you?"

She shakes her head. "No. It's really dangerous. We see children and teens in the ER all the time with concussions, most of which are sport related, especially from football. There are so many studies now about concussions and worse. Michael's my baby. He's all I have."

"I know, but you have to let him live. Life isn't life if it's spent playing it safe."

Melanie shoots me a look that makes her disapproval very clear. "Should I let him jump out of an airplane for his birthday? He actually asked me for that last week."

"How about within reason?" Without thinking, I reach out and take Melanie's hand in mine. "You have time to think about it. It's too late for him to play tackle this season. Maybe he'll change his mind by next fall and be interested in something else, or you can compromise and let him play flag football in the spring. It'll all work out."

"I don't want him to get hurt."

"I see the look in his eyes when he talks about football. That isn't going away easily. There are risks involved in everything we do. If playing football makes Michael happy, you should let him play."

"I guess so." Melanie speaks quietly, like she's trying to convince herself to believe me.

I watch my thumb as it moves over the back of Melanie's hand in little circles. Memories of our kiss earlier today flood my mind. She tasted so incredibly good. I wish I didn't know that, but at the same time, that's the best memory I can think of right now. My gaze lifts from our clasped hands to Melanie's eyes.

"I meant what I said earlier this afternoon. I'm not good for you."

She nods slightly and leans a little closer. "Did you ever think that I might be good for you?" And she could be. She already has been good for me. "You just gave me this big speech about how we should do the things that make us happy. Kissing you right now would make me happy."

Melanie doesn't wait to study my reaction. Her lips touch mine softly.

I'm done for.

Everything about Melanie makes me want to make her mine. My tongue does just that. My hands move to either side of her jaw to hold her still so I can kiss her fully.

And I do.

I hold back every reservation and nagging doubt and just *feel*.

I feel the soft skin of her neck against my palms.

I feel the touch of her hands behind my head as she pulls me even closer.

I feel the vibration of the noise she makes deep in her throat.

And I feel the touch of her tongue against mine. Want and sheer need flow through me. Man, it would be incredible to make love with this woman. My body responds with a shudder. I bring my hands to Melanie's waist and tug. In one movement, she straddles my lap.

She's right there, her middle pressing against mine, with only a few layers of fabric between us.

Could this really happen?

Melanie pulls back slowly, her breaths heavy. Her eyes are much darker than normal, almost chocolate. The corners of her mouth tip up slightly into an almost smile.

Can she actually want me? My brain registers this seedling of doubt. Does she have any idea what a mess I am? That's all it takes for the seed to take root and grow.

Melanie's attracted to me. That's all. She doesn't understand. She doesn't know what a mess I am, and she doesn't know what a mess I can make of her life. Michael's, too. I only want us to be friends, but I'm not strong enough to keep my hands off of her.

Mel pulls back and looks at me.

"Why are you afraid of me?"

"I'm not." I'm terrified.

"I'm a big girl, you know."

I shrug. Really mature. "I already explained. I'm a walking disaster. I don't want to hurt you and Michael."

"You won't."

"I'm leaving in three weeks."

Melanie recovers quickly, but there's no missing the grimace that was her first reaction. She leans to the side until she falls off my lap and lands on the couch next to me. She doesn't move away. Instead, she sits sideways on the cushion next to mine.

"I didn't know you had an end date in mind for this trip, but I knew you'd be leaving at some point. You live in Florida or wherever the Marines send you."

The Marines won't be sending me anywhere, seeing as I'm no longer active duty. I keep that to myself. I don't want Melanie getting any ideas, no matter how farfetched, that I will extend my stay.

"I think I should go." I look straight ahead as I lean forward and stand up. Eye contact would be a bad idea, a thought that's justified as soon as I turn and see the hurt in Melanie's eyes. She looks away quickly and brings her hands together in her lap. What the hell is wrong with me? I tell myself I need to leave so I don't hurt her, and all that happens is that I hurt her anyway. I liked it so much better when her eyes were full of need. Now, my burning need is to get out of this house.

Chapter Thirteen

Melanie

The pitter-patter of the raindrops against the window lulls me in and out of sleep. I roll over and drift off again, the warmth of my bed much preferred to the frosty cold that I'm sure to find outside. The forecast called for chilly rain beginning overnight. Apparently, they got it right. I know because I was awake at two o'clock when the rain first started.

Why does this have to be so difficult? I like Will. I know Will likes me. What's the problem? Those are the thoughts that kept me awake until the wee hours. So he's only here for a few weeks. So what? We're both adults. I have no unrealistic expectations.

Sure, I like him, and maybe I could grow to like him a lot. It seems like we deserve a chance. When he kissed me last night—I don't even have words to describe what my body felt like. *Hot*. That's one word that comes to mind, but it was more than that. It was like liquid heat somehow, moving around inside of me until every nook and cranny was on fire. Molten lava? That sounds cheesy and more like a way to die—not the amazing feeling I felt in Will's arms and straddling his—yeah, he likes me, too. Let's just leave it at that.

With a big sigh, I fling the covers off of me and heave myself out of bed. Yep, it's chilly in here. I grab my robe and slippers and head straight for the thermostat in the hallway. I turn it up a couple degrees, and the heat kicks on right away.

Michael's door is halfway open, just the way he likes it and just the way I left it when Will and I brought him up to bed last night. I peek inside. He's awake of course. He's an early riser, and it's almost eight o'clock, so that isn't a surprise. Michael sits up in his bed with a pencil in his hand and a pad of paper lying on his lap. He's drawing something. I step closer.

"Good morning, sweet pea. How are you this morning?"

"Hi, Mommy." My heart squeezes as Michael looks up at me and smiles. He has Malcolm's smile, but it looks better on Michael, for sure. I step closer to his bed, so I can see his work.

"What are you drawing?"

The words are out of my mouth before I look down and see for myself. I know exactly what it is. There are blotches of golds, reds, and oranges and two figures standing on green grass. Michael's a pretty decent artist for a four-year-old, but even if he wasn't, this one would be easy to figure out. He looks up at me and smiles.

"I'm making this for Will. Do you think he'll like it?"

"I'm sure he'll love it. How about some pancakes and sausage for breakfast?"

"Yum," is Michael's only response before he chooses an orange pencil and dives back into his project.

I lean down and kiss him on the forehead. "I'll call you when breakfast is ready."

Two hours later, our tummies are full, and the rain has started to let up. It's still raining, but it's reduced to a soaking kind of rain instead of the all-out gushing of the early morning. Thank goodness ,because I was reminded every time I looked out the front window that my gutters are clogged. It's not exactly a surprise since I've cleaned them out like never. It's on the part of my to-do list that keeps getting pushed off to another day and then another. It's kind of like the bulb that was burned out in the   backyard flood light that Will replaced. I plan to do these things someday, but that day never comes.

"Can we go give my drawing to Will?"

I can't stop my sigh. I'm sure Will would like to see it, but I don't know if I'm ready to see him yet. No, I'm ready to see Will. I just don't think Will is ready to see me.

"Is something wrong, Mommy?"

"Oh, of course not, sweetie. I don't want your picture to get wet. Why don't we visit with Bunny first? Hopefully, the rain will have stopped by the time we get home."

Michael's expression turns thoughtful. He glances out the large window that takes up most of one of the walls of our family room. "Okay. Do you think Will is gonna like my picture?"

"I think Will's going to love it. I bet he'll put it on the refrigerator with the pictures you made for Bunny."

That gets a smile. Michael begins chatting happily about the seven pieces of his artwork that Bunny has posted to her refrigerator. He remembers each one in detail. The discussion lasts the entire way to the rehabilitation center, which is really only a five-minute drive.

Michael and I pull the hoods of our raincoats up onto our heads, hold hands, and jog through the parking lot to the front door of the facility, laughing all the way. The rain is definitely chilly, but still, there's just something fun about running through the rain.

We take some deep breaths to quiet ourselves before walking down the hall toward the patient rooms. It's only eleven o'clock in the morning. Some of these people might still be sleeping, especially on a dreary day like this. Others, though, like Bunny, have been awake since the early morning.

I hear Bunny's voice carry out into the hallway. Someone's in there with her. I take a deep breath to steel myself in case it's Will. I can handle seeing him again. I even *want* to see him again. I just want to make sure I can handle however Will decides to handle seeing me again. This is getting complicated.

Will isn't here.

Granny Simms sits in the rocking chair next to Bunny's recliner. There's a huge dark purple splotch around her left eye, which is only partially open. What the heck?

"Granny!" Michael shouts ecstatically and takes off in a run. She only has three grandchildren of her own—Hunter and his siblings—but everyone calls her that. "Granny? What happened to your eye?"

Granny pulls Michael to her for a tight hug. She releases him, and he gets another one from Bunny. I walk closer until I'm only a few feet from the women.

"Yeah, Granny, what did happen to your eye? I saw Kate yesterday, and she didn't mention anything about this."

Granny sighs. "There was an incident last night after bingo." I feel myself grimace for poor Kate, dealing with Granny's shenanigans. I feel relief and guilt at the same time. I'm so glad I didn't accept Kate's invitation to bingo but feel guilty that I wasn't there to help her with God only knows what happened to cause that shiner on Granny's eye.

"Well?" I'm dying to know. Granny is in her seventies, at least. If she has a black eye, there has to be a good story to go with it.

"I had my luckiest night at bingo ever. I won three regular games—although I did have to split one of the pots with Roger Davenport. Everyone was getting very grumbly at the fact that I was winning so much. Then, there were a few people who actually booed when I won the jackpot at the end of the night. I guess I learned who my true friends are, mind you. See, in total, I'd won seven hundred and fifty dollars. That's the most I've ever won at bingo in a single night. I'm there almost every stinking Saturday, and most of the time I come home empty-handed. You'd think these people would be kindhearted enough to be happy for me."

"You'd think so," Bunny chimes in with a firm nod.

"How did your winnings lead to a black eye?"

"Kate, Frank, and I were walking to the car afterwards. We were talking about going to Minnie's Diner to celebrate. Then, out of nowhere, comes Gertie Cooper. Do you know what she did?" Granny's on fire now. The indignation drips from her pores. Does she really want me to answer her question? I guess not because she continues. "She accused me of cheating right then and there. She said that the bingo caller, Stan, and I had worked out an arrangement where he called the numbers I needed to win. Have you ever heard of such a thing?"

Um. No, but then I've hardly ever been to bingo. Granny seems like she really wants an answer this time, so I manage a shake of my head.

"Gertie went on and on about how she needed G-55 to win the jackpot, and that was the hard luck number, so she was extra ticked off. I don't mean to be rude, but the next number that would have been called if someone hadn't won is called the hard luck number for a reason. Honestly."

"Then what happened?" Michael asks this time. Geez. He probably shouldn't be hearing any of this, but it's too late to stop it at this point.

"Gertie hit me in the eye with her handbag!"

A gasp comes out of my mouth involuntarily. Obviously, it had to be something, but come on. Gertie Cooper is in her fifties. She's a grandmother, and she sings in her church choir. This is unreal.

"What would possess Gertie to hit you?"

"Bingo is serious business."

"What did you do after she hit you? Did you fall down? Did you injure anything else?"

Granny sits even straighter in her chair. "I did not fall down," she says proudly. "I stood my ground and clocked Gertie right in the face. And I didn't use my purse either. No, I did not. I used my fist. I'm normally opposed to violence, but what was I supposed to do? I was attacked and had to defend myself." She smiles wryly. "I'm sure she looks worse than me today. I already heard from three people that Gertie didn't make it to church this morning."

"What did Frank and Kate think about all this?" Again, poor Kate.

"Kate got in between us before I could get another hit in. Gertie was crying like a baby. Her friend Althea called the police. Hunter came with that young man, Bryce Chambers. He's such a cutie. It's a good thing Bryce was there because Hunter had to recuse himself from dealing with any of it. Gertie was calling foul play about that, too. Can I help it if my grandson is a policeman? I mean, honestly."

"How was Hunter?"

"Fuming mad, of course, but it wasn't *my* fault. It was self-defense, and I have witnesses. June Carlson and Jimmy Morgan saw the whole thing. They gave their statements to Bryce, so I didn't get taken into jail or anything. Geez, I think Gertie's the one who should have been arrested. I was just walking to the car, minding my own business, when I was attacked. What is this world coming to?"

I can't help but feel bad for poor Kate about her part in this situation, but the mental picture of these two ladies duking it out in the fire station parking lot is too much. Before long, we're all laughing hysterically. Michael, too. I'm not sure he even understands what took place, but he gets right into it and begins laughing harder than the rest of us. Maybe laughter really is infectious.

"You must have the gossip circles buzzing like crazy this morning."

"Oh, don't you know it. I've had to turn my cell phone off to stop it from ringing. Let's talk about the other gossip that I heard this morning."

"What's that?"

"I heard that a certain young man had dinner with you and Michael last night."

Um. I swear I feel the color drain from my face.

"Will coming over for dinner last night is news?"

Bunny smiles. "Will visited earlier this morning and was here when Beverly arrived. He mentioned that he went to your house for dinner. That's all."

"That is all. It isn't gossip-worthy."

My cheeks must have regained some color because they now feel like they're on fire and likely giving me away. I'm sticking with my story anyway. Not much happened, so it isn't worthy of being categorized as gossip.

"Aw, honey," Granny says quietly. "I didn't mean to get you upset. I'm telling you, though, that Will is a major piece of man-candy. You have to see that."

Both of the ladies study me, but I'm not giving them an inch. I plead the fifth.

Bunny smiles a small smile. "I don't think I can

use that term to describe my own nephew, but I can say that Will is a handsome young man. He always has been. He's been through a lot and needs something good in his life."

I have to say something. "Maybe he does need something good in his life, but I don't think he's looking for me." *Unfortunately.* "Can we move on to a different subject now?"

Granny's smile grows, and she turns to Bunny. "I've saved the best news for last. I'm going to be a great-granny."

Bunny clasps her hands together. "Kate's going to have a baby?"

The conversation carries on from there because no one can compete with the news of a baby.

Chapter Fourteen

Will

This is probably the last thing I should be doing in my current state of exhaustion, but it needs to be done, and I deserve the hassle. The rain has been coming down hard since the wee hours, and since daylight, I've been watching the rainwater spill over Melanie's clogged gutter instead of into it. Now that the rain has calmed down some and Melanie and Michael left the house for a while, I can get it cleaned out.

I breathe in another deep breath of cool fall air. Fresh air is just what I need after one hell of a migraine and then a visit with Aunt Bunny. She's really starting to look better. The doctor says she could be coming home soon. She sure doesn't need to see me like this. I should be taking care of her, not the other way around.

Her friend, Granny, is a total hoot.

She and Granny were so thrilled at first to hear I had dinner with Melanie last night. Then I bummed them out when I told them nothing's going to happen between the two of us. They didn't believe me at first, and maybe they still don't, but I can't let them get their hopes up. I'm not in any place to offer myself to anyone, especially Melanie and Michael.

I wrote about my situation with Melanie for a couple hours last night. I wrote until I'd filled an entire spiral notebook. I made a list of the pros and cons of Melanie and me as a couple. That did not work out in my favor. I wrote random thoughts with the hope of discovering some idea of how we might have a future together. All my writing efforts were for naught. The conclusion was just as I thought it would be—I'm in no shape to be anything to anyone right now, especially to people as special as Melanie and Michael.

Why does this have to be so disgusting? I pull out another handful of blackened nastiness and let it fall to the ground. I deserve this kind of work today, anything to try and make up for the look on Melanie's face when I walked out on her last night. *Again*. Sure, this job could be worse, but as house maintenance goes, cleaning gutters sucks. I've always had apartments, and Mom and Dad have palm trees in their front yard—not the kind of tree that sheds little leaves and clogs things up with this disgusting brown decay. *Whatever*. I deserve this and worse, not only for walking out on Melanie in the first place, but also for being too much of a wimp to apologize.

I get back inside Aunt Bunny's house just in time to see Melanie pull into her driveway. She'd have been pissed for sure if she'd caught me out there working on her house. My head is starting to throb again. Maybe an interrogation by Bunny and her friend and then manual labor were too much after that doozy of a headache. I climb out of my wet clothes, grab a glass of water, and head to bed to rest and hopefully keep the migraine from coming back full force.

Visions of Melanie are there as soon as I close my eyes. I let them come.

Chapter Fifteen

Melanie

"If you didn't want me to go with you, you could have just told me. You didn't have to sneak away."

Will turns his gaze downward to avoid eye contact. I can't say as I blame him. I tried to keep the anger out of my voice, and I mostly did. It would have been a lot worse this morning. I was infuriated when I came home from taking Michael to preschool to find that Will had left for the doctor without me. I spent the time sitting on the couch reading a book, but what I was really doing was staring out the window waiting for him to come home. I met him in the garage before he had a chance to shut the door.

"Are you mad?" He braves a look at me, and I

immediately forgive him. His eyes are so sad. His shoulders slump. He looks like he's been pulled through the ringer, which is why I wanted to go with him in the first place. With a big sigh, I remove my hands from my hips and step closer. "I was trying to avoid you seeing me like this."

I pull Will to me for a hug. Not only does he let me, he holds on tight. The thump-thump of his heartbeat echoes through me. It isn't the moment of fire that we shared Saturday night. It's the warmth of the embrace, the softness of his sweater, and the hardness of his chest. It's the need to be here for Will.

Being here for him now also means letting him get some rest. I pull back and break our embrace.

"Do you need to get some sleep?"

"Maybe later, but for now, I'm starving. Will you come out with me and show me one of the local spots?"

"Really?"

The corners of his mouth lift up to form a shy smile. "Really. The last thing I need right now is to sit here alone in this house."

"Okay. I know the perfect place."

Minnie's Diner is just what its name implies—great food without putting on any airs. If you want fancy, there's Leslie's sandwich shop. They use croissants for some of their sandwiches. For lunch, at least, that's the fanciest you can get around here.

We arrive just before one o'clock, late enough to miss the lunch rush. The board announces fried chicken as the Tuesday special. It hardly needs to be advertised. The daily special's been the same for as long as I can remember.

I know I can't go to Minnie's without seeing someone I know. Today, the someones are Hunter and Bryce. *Great.* I haven't seen them since the embarrassing events in Bunny's back yard. Tyler's with them, too. Hopefully there isn't any crime happening right now since most of the police force is having lunch.

Hunter stands and gives me a quick hug when he sees me. I say hello to the others. "You all remember Will." Bryce clamps down a smirk. I feel the heat on my face. So embarrassing. "Tyler, you missed all the action the other night. This is Will Everton. Will, this is Tyler McMann." They shake hands.

"I heard about it. Glad you're okay."

Tyler's grin is huge. He looks like a movie star when he smiles like that. Those blue eyes and blond locks really work for him. Other than a general appreciation of his good looks, I've never had any feelings for him. Which is good, considering he is now married to my friend Meg.

Will is much more my type—darker hair and eyes. He returns Tyler's smile with one of his own. My knees go weak.

"Melanie packs quite a punch. Thank goodness I'm on her good side now."

Time for a change of topic.

"Hunter here is my friend Kate's husband."

Will nods. "Ahh. I hear congratulations are in order. Very good news."

"Thanks. I think Kate's told just about everyone in town."

"And your Granny. I met her the other day. She's something."

Everyone shares a laugh. A good time to excuse ourselves.

"We'll see you all later."

"One more thing. Do you fish? Kate's brother, Brady, and I are going fishing on Friday. Would you like to join us?"

Will's face lights up. "I love to fish, although I don't get much chance to do it."

"Great. We'll come pick you up about seven Friday morning. There's a pond up by the Richardson family cabin that has some trout and the occasional bass."

"Sounds great. Nice to meet you all."

Will still wears a smile when we take our seats across from each other in a nearby booth.

"Everyone here is so nice."

"They are. Davidson was a great place to grow up. That's why I want Michael to grow up here, too."

"With my dad being in the Marines, we moved around a lot when I was a kid. What's it like to live in the same place your whole life?"

"I did go away to school. I went to college and nursing school in Richmond. The city life was fine, but it isn't for me. I like knowing my neighbors. Bunny, for example, is the best. I'm so glad that we live next door to her. I think it was fate. She helped me a lot when Malcolm left us." Why did I bring that up? Moving on. "I like running into people I know when I go out."

"So you always have to get dolled up to leave the house?"

I smile. "Yeah, maybe that isn't always the best. There's also the downside that everyone knows your business. There aren't many secrets in a town this small."

"That could get old."

"Yep. For example, see that couple sitting over there? They are my parents' neighbors. And I'm sure she'll tell my mom about seeing me here with you the second she gets home. If she texted, my mom would already know, but I don't think Mrs. Faulkner has embraced the art of texting."

"What will your mom think of the news?"

I shrug. "I'm not sure." Not entirely true. I know my Mom will wish I had been here with Malcolm. "Dad will be happy. He likes you."

"I'll have to work on your mom."

That, I was not expecting. Will quickly closes his mouth, as if trying to stop any more words from being released. Our waitress picks this moment to place our fried chicken in front of us. She refills our glasses of sweet tea and hurries away to help others in need of grease and sugar.

"Sorry. I shouldn't have said that. I must be driving you crazy."

"What do you mean?"

"Obviously, I like you, Melanie. A lot." A warmth begins in my chest. "I can't help it. But, what I said before is still true. I'm not capable of a relationship right now. I'm a mess. My brain tells me to stay away from you, yet I'm glad that you're with me right now."

"How about you concentrate on getting yourself better, and I'll concentrate on us being friends?"

"That isn't fair to you."

"Don't put so much pressure on yourself. I like spending time with you, and so does Michael. I don't expect anything more from you."

"I'll have to go back."

"I know. For now, eat up, and then I'll show you Davidson's pride and joy."

Chapter Sixteen

Will

I see him before Melanie does.

Malcolm.

He walks into the diner as if he owns the place, a petite blonde on his arm. Seemingly unaffected by my stare, he saunters in the direction of our table. Melanie notices and turns to see him. She gasps quietly. Her look of surprise is schooled by the time the couple makes it to our table.

Melanie is the first to speak. "Ellen, what are doing with *him*?"

The woman doesn't answer. Instead, she smiles coyly and looks up at Malcolm. Malcolm smiles as well, although his comes off as creepy. His pores drip asshole.

"Do you think because you gave up on a good thing, everyone else should as well? Ellen, here, was nice enough to point out a few things that I was missing with you. If you'd rather slum it with *this guy,* then you go ahead. My relationship with Ellen, however, does not mean I no longer want to know *my* son."

Melanie's face flares a deep and immediate red. "Michael is no longer your son. You made sure of that when we divorced. You'll never know him."

I stand and face Malcolm. "You're making Melanie uncomfortable. It would be best if you leave."

Malcolm stands a little straighter. His nostrils flare. He's good and pissed, but you know what, so am I.

"Everything okay over here?"

Hunter and Bryce stand next to me. I was so focused on Malcolm, I didn't notice anything else. No longer do they look like a joyful group out for lunch. The serious expressions, straight stances, not to mention their uniforms, paint a picture of full authority.

Malcolm answers. "Everything's fine. We just came in to grab some lunch."

"I think it would be a good idea if you go somewhere else to eat."

Before Malcolm can argue his point, Melanie speaks. "No, we'll go. Will and I are finished anyway."

She stands from her seat and pushes her shoulders back before throwing money on the table to cover the bill. "Let's go, Will." She grabs my hand and pulls me out the door.

We turn to the right and walk on the sidewalk toward downtown. I squeeze her hand tighter into mine. She squeezes back. The red tint of her cheeks has calmed to a light pink. I think the fresh air is good for both of us.

"You didn't have to leave, you know. Hunter was going to make them go."

"I know. I just wanted out of there. I could feel the stares of everyone in the place, and I didn't want to give them any more to talk about. Sorry if I made you leave before you finished lunch."

"Although that was the best fried chicken I've ever had, it's a good thing we left."

"Why is that?"

"Because now I can buy you a milkshake at the General Store."

"That's where we're headed, actually. You know about the milkshakes there?"

"They were my favorite part of visiting Aunt Bunny when I was a kid. She'd take me there to get a milkshake and buy me a bag of candy to take home. Do they still have barrels and bins of candy to choose from?"

That gets a smile. Who doesn't smile when they think about candy?

"They do. Michael loves it there, just like I did

when I was a kid. Of course, it was even better for me because Kate's parents owned the store then. I got free candy all the time. It was a child's dream."

"No more free candy for you, then?"

"Actually, I suppose I could have all the free candy I want. I just can't eat it anymore. Kate runs the store now."

We pause for a moment to look at the store window. It's like the fall exploded. There are pumpkins and gourds placed on straw. A smiling scarecrow sits on a hay bale with a bucket of candy in his lap. I feel excited to go inside. I haven't been here yet since coming to Davidson. I'm not sure why not. I have plenty of happy memories here.

A little bell jingles to announce our arrival. Melanie's friend, Kate, pops her head up from behind the long counter. Her smile grows at the sight of us.

"Hi there. Be right with you."

Melanie pulls me straight to the soda fountain that sits against the far wall. It looks almost exactly like it did when Aunt Bunny brought me here twenty-some years ago. It's a kid's dream come true. Four stools line the stainless steel counter. Glass jars of candy stand in a row next to a small glass case showing off two kinds of cones.

"Chocolate or vanilla?"

Melanie drops my hand and moves behind the counter.

"Is this self-service?"

"It is for me. I worked here some in high school. I promise it will still be delicious."

I take a seat on one of the stools.

"I'm sure it will be. Chocolate, please."

"Good choice."

While Melanie gets to work on making our milkshakes, I check out the store. As a kid, I was only interested in the candy, ice cream, and toys. From my seat, I can also see craft supplies, bakeware, gardening supplies, and bait and tackle. Which reminds me, I need to see what kind of fishing equipment I can come up with for my pending fishing trip with Hunter and his friend. I might have to come back here and get some supplies.

"Everything good with you two today?" Kate asks the question, but it's clear things aren't good with her.

"We're okay." Melanie's words are laced with concern. She stares at her friend as if waiting for Kate to say something.

"Mom told me you know about her appointment with Dr. Hanover."

Melanie nods and then brings Kate in for a hug. Whatever is happening is clearly not good. Melanie releases Kate. Both women have tears in their eyes.

"Dr. Hanover is a great doctor. He'll take good care of her. Sorry that I knew about this before you did and didn't tell you. Your mom made me promise to keep quiet because she wanted to be the one to tell you."

"I know. I have to run into the back and check on something. You guys take all the time you need." Kate embraces Melanie one last time and disappears through a nearby door into the back of the store.

"What's wrong with Kate's mother?"

"Ovarian cancer." Meg sighs quietly. "Dr. Hanover really is a great doctor, and they found the cancer early. Everything's going to be okay."

Chapter Seventeen

Melanie

Michael's face lights up brightly at the sight of Will. I didn't plan to bring Will with me to pick Michael up from preschool, but the timing was such that I didn't have a choice. Michael runs to us, grabs Will by the hand, and pulls him into the classroom. I find Will surrounded by children from Michael's class as Michael speaks excitedly about leaves and football.

Will seems perfectly at ease with all the attention. He answers question after question until I'm finally able to drag the two of them out of there. Michael buckles up into his car seat, and we head home.

"My birthday is on Saturday. Can you come to my party, Will?"

I hold my breath, awaiting Will's response. It's not necessary.

"I'll try, buddy. I love a good party," Will answers without any hesitation at all.

I can't take it anymore. Ellen has ignored me all morning. This is ridiculous.

"Ellen, may I speak with you alone for a moment?"

She looks up at me and tilts her head to the side. "I doubt we have anything to discuss."

My hands move to my hips. "I would appreciate it if you would give me a moment of your time." What's wrong with this woman? I'm trying to help her.

She sighs, stands, and walks into one of the empty patient rooms. With a small sigh, I follow her. She turns to face me and folds her arms over her chest. What has gotten into her?

"Is this because you're jealous? Because Malcolm picked me over you?"

Condescension and utter snootiness roll off her. This is not the woman I've worked with for the last few years. I take a deep breath and try to calm down before I say something I'll regret.

"First of all, I'm not jealous. I do not want Malcolm back."

"That's what he said you'd say."

"What? Listen, I want to warn you to stay away from him."

Her blue eyes flash. "So you are jealous?"

"No, not for that reason. You need to be careful with him. He's not the sweet person he pretends to be. He left me when he found out I was pregnant. Is that the kind of man you want?"

She rolls her eyes. This is going nowhere fast. "Malcolm made a mistake. He admits that. That's why he's back in town. He wants to have a relationship with his son. You should stop being such a bitch and let him. Maybe you drove him away."

Seriously?

"Look, I don't know what Malcolm's up to, but you can't trust anything he says. He was just at my house on Saturday professing his love for me." Ellen's eyes widen as she inhales a quick breath. "I'm not trying to make you mad. I only want to warn you. He's up to something. Don't trust him."

"Maybe it's you who's up to something. You're just trying to turn everyone against him. That's not fair."

Not fair?

"I tried. Good luck to you. I hope you're very happy."

I'm out. I leave Ellen standing in the little room. I tried to warn her. Obviously, Malcolm's got her good. My only hope is that she'll think things over and figure some of this out on her own.

Why is Malcolm dating her? If he's trying to make me jealous, his plan is completely backfiring. But, despite Ellen's behavior toward me, I don't want her to get hurt.

I notice the fresh layer of mulch the second I pull into the driveway.

Will did more work at my house. I never mentioned needing new mulch, of all things. Sure, it'll look put-together for Michael's party and all, but it wasn't necessary. Is this Will's way of apologizing for going to his doctor appointment without me?

Chapter Eighteen

Will

"Do you always have this much good fortune when fishing?"

Brady grins from ear to ear as he shows off yet another large bass. The early afternoon sun shines brightly on his deep red hair, making it appear almost orange. Most men wouldn't be able to pull off red hair and the pale skin that goes with it. Brady somehow manages to look rugged despite his unfortunate coloring.

Hunter answers my question. "We usually do well up here, but we're doing especially great today."

"We picked a good day to do this," Brady adds. "A perfect, sunny fall day. Apparently, the fish like this weather as much as we do."

The day is beautiful. The early morning frost has given way to warm sunshine. The trees that line the pond are all adorned in hues of gold, yellow, red, and orange.

Brady adds his latest catch to the cooler. "Hopefully, Hunter, you and Kate will have a boy who'll come with us on these fishing trips."

"Girls fish too."

"Some girls do. Kate fished here when she was younger. Then she got all girly and grew out of it."

Hunter shrugs.

"Did you all grow up together? Melanie talks about what a great place this was to grow up."

Hunter and Brady share a look. Some kind of communication passes between them.

"Kate and I went to school together after my family moved here when I was in the second grade. We weren't friends." Hunter's tone makes it clear that there's much more to the story. I don't ask, and my patience pays off when he continues. "I've been in love with Kate all that time, but we didn't get along."

"Really?"

"We found each other again last year, and we're making up for lost time."

Brady chuckles. "That you are. Married and pregnant in less than a year."

"When it's right, it's right." Hunter turns to me. "Speaking of which, how are things going with you and Mel?"

Um.

Opening up my personal life to men who are practically strangers is not exactly something I do. I struggle to come up with an answer that isn't too personal but isn't rude either.

"I get it if you don't want to share, and I don't mean to pry. It's just that Granny told me that you were at Mel's house for dinner on Saturday, and you were together again at Minnie's for lunch."

Hunter stops as if this is enough of an explanation.

Brady picks up where Hunter left off. "Mel's been through an awful lot. She could use some happiness in her life."

A sigh escapes. "I do like Melanie. A lot. The problem is that I'm not in a good place right now."

"Granny filled us in on that, too."

Great.

"I know it sounds like a lot of gossip, and with Granny involved, some of it is. Davidson is a small town. People know things."

"Well, what have you heard about me?"

"We heard you're a hero, that you saved someone in Iraq." I don't know about the hero part, but I give Hunter a small nod of acknowledgement. "We also heard that you're suffering from PTSD since coming back to the states."

I nod again. "I'm having a hard time getting the images of that day to go away. They visit me almost every night. They're so vivid, it's like I'm there reliving the experience over and over."

"That sucks."

"Pretty much. It feels good to get out and do something else. Thanks for inviting me along today."

Hunter smiles and pats my shoulder. "It's good to have you along. Now, if you can catch another fish, you'll have enough to make Melanie and Michael dinner tonight."

I smile and close my eyes in hopes of memorizing this moment so I can write about it tonight. I want to remember all of it—the warmth of the sun, the happiness of catching dinner, the feeling of getting away from my life for a few hours. It's been a great day.

Chapter Nineteen

Melanie

Another Friday almost done. Goodness knows it's been quite a week. Besides wanting to get the hell away from Ellen, I love the idea of two full days at home with Michael and, hopefully, Will. The radio crackles with an alert. An ambulance is coming in with a patient—a pedestrian hit by a car. Not life threatening. Thank you, God. One bad thing about working in the only hospital in town is that you personally know many of the patients. That's not always a good thing.

A smiling vision of Will pops into my mind. I've thought about him more often today than I want to admit. Did he have fun on his fishing trip? Will he feel well enough to attend Michael's birthday party tomorrow? Does Will spend as much time thinking about me as I do thinking about him?

My cell phone buzzes, bringing me out of my thoughts. A photo of Hunter taken at his rehearsal dinner flashes on my screen. My nerves tighten at the sight. Hunter doesn't call me without a reason.

"Hi, Hunter. Everything okay?"

"Sort-of. I just got a call from McMann. An ambulance is bringing Will in now. He was out walking and was hit by a car."

My heart drops to my stomach. "How bad is it?" I ask the question despite the fact that I've already heard his condition isn't life threatening. Still, Will is hurt.

"I don't think it's too bad. He's conscious. I'm on my way in now myself to check it out."

"Thanks, Hunter."

I disconnect and choke back the panic. I'm a nurse, and I'm on duty. I have to keep my cool. My legs feel too heavy to move from my spot near the desk, but I will them to move anyway and run toward the emergency door. I arrive just as the ambulance pulls in. Matt Foster climbs from the driver's seat and yanks open the back doors. I'm there in a flash.

He's awake.

He's breathing.

So silly for me to even have these thoughts. Hunter told me Will was conscious, so of course he's alive. Of course he's breathing. Still, seeing it for myself is something else altogether. My chest pounds hard, echoing my relief.

The EMTs remove Will from the ambulance. Our eyes meet. Will gives me a small smile.

"I told them I didn't need an ambulance. They insisted I take it."

Tears threaten. I take a deep breath and beg them to stay inside. I'm a professional. I can't go all weepy at the site of a neighbor being brought into the hospital on a stretcher.

But Will's more than a neighbor.

One stubborn tear slides down my cheek. Will pushes it away. "I'm fine. Really. The poor woman who hit me's in much worse shape than I am."

I turn to Matt. "Who hit him?"

"Poor Mrs. Butterfield. She's with the police now."

"Oh no." Mrs. Butterfield is a super-sweet elderly woman who lives a couple streets over from me. "Is she hurt?"

"Just emotionally. She's really torn up about running into your friend, here. I guess I can call him that now, given how distraught you looked when we got here. Kind of a big change from a couple weeks ago when we were at your house." Anger rolls around with the anxiety in the pit of my stomach until I look up to see Matt's shy grin. I lift one side of my lip and flare my nose in his direction. A very mature response to his mature comment.

"Let's get Will inside and get him checked out."

A shout gets me on my feet and running to him. The full moon provides enough light to see that Will's sleeping. He mumbles something else and rolls over. A small sigh escapes me as I step closer to the bed to get a better view of the man sleeping in my guest room.

Will's hair is mussed, and his chest is bare. I squint to take in what I can, wishing I could turn on the light for a better view. I didn't plan on gawking at him like this when I insisted he stay with me tonight. I admit there was a little bit of selfishness in my offer. I was worried about him, and having him here with me makes me feel somewhat better. The poor man was hit by a Buick. He was downed by a bomb in Iraq, smashed in the head with a flashlight, and then hit with Mrs. Butterfield's bumper. It's too much for anyone to take.

And seeing Will stretched out on a gurney was too much for me to take. It was all I could do not to fall apart right then and there. I'm so thankful I was on duty though. I was able to be there with him and hold his hand when Dr. Simmons checked him out. That might have been more for my sake than Will's, but nevertheless, I was there to do it.

When my shift ended, I stayed. Mom was happy to have Michael stay with her and Dad for a sleepover tonight. That was a very good thing because it took a while to get Will through the tests and allow the doctor to observe him enough to discharge him into my care. It took a little convincing to get Will to stay here with me, but he finally relented. I had hoped he'd be more comfortable here. He clearly isn't. Is this what it's like for him every night? Rolling around and talking doesn't make for a good night's rest.

"Get down!" The shout causes me to jump. I land on my feet in time for Will to grab my hand and pull me into the bed. "Are you out of your mind standing there in the open?" Will covers my body with his, leaving me breathless. "You're going to get us killed."

He's dreaming.

The shock of being pinned under Will's hard body quickly turns into something else as his legs connect with mine. Is he…?

Will isn't just bare-chested. Will is naked.

There is a nude man on top of me. How did this happen? He was dressed when I put him to bed.

Relax. I'm a nurse. Nude men aren't supposed to have an effect on me.

But then, my patients are never pressed against me like this.

My cheeks warm first, and then the heat spreads to my middle. My body aches with remembrance. It's been way too long since I've been this close to a man. There's been no one since Malcolm. I would love nothing more than to make love with Will but not like this. Will isn't really here. As far as he knows, he's back in Iraq reliving his nightmare over again.

That doesn't mean I don't feel the weight of him pressing on me. The amazing feeling of his body on top of mine. Another flare of heat flashes through me.

Will flinches and mumbles something I can't make out.

Please don't let him wake up and find us in this position.

Too late.

Will's eyelashes flutter. "What?" He jumps back in surprise and slides off of me.

I can't exactly slink away. "You, um, had a bad dream." I move my gaze away from Will's eyes. My nightshirt has ridden up to reveal my bare legs and panties. Heat flushes my cheeks again.

"Did I hurt you?"

"No, of course not. I think you were trying to protect me." His dark eyes, so full of anguish, meet mine. "Will." The word leaves my mouth as a whisper.

His eyes darken. He closes the distance between us. His lips brush mine softly. Electricity sparks from this small touch. He pulls away to judge my reaction. My body flushes with heat as I wait in anticipation for his next move. Then it happens. His lips descend on mine, hard and demanding. His hands are everywhere all at once—on my neck, my breasts, my stomach. Will moves on top of me again. Sweet heaven, he feels so good. He breaks our kiss and looks at me with eyes so full of desire that I'm more breathless than ever. His hands slide down my sides to my hips taking my panties with them. Will positions himself on top of me. Our eyes lock, and then he's inside me.

Our gaze holds as we move together in perfect rhythm. "Mel." Although it's more of a moan than a word, it's the last thing I hear before we go over the edge together. I know I may never be the same again.

Chapter Twenty

Will

I knew being with Melanie would be amazing. I've been dreaming of what this experience would be like almost since the first moment I met her. My imagination didn't come close to the real thing— what it was like to move with her, to come with her, to look at her and to see the need in her eyes.

I lean on my elbows to support some of my weight. As incredible as Melanie's body feels beneath mine, I don't want to crush her.

"Wait. Don't go."

"I'm not going anywhere." I bring my lips to hers again for a soft kiss. "How did this happen exactly, you being here in bed with me?"

"You were shouting. I came to check on you, and you pulled me into bed with you."

I close my mouth and swallow down a curse. "Did I hurt you?"

"No, I already told you." Melanie shakes her head as if to emphasize her answer. I touch her hair softly and tuck a stray piece behind her ear. "You didn't hurt me. You were trying to protect me from something. You covered me with your body, and that's when you woke up."

Melanie's rose-colored cheeks, already flushed from our lovemaking, redden even more.

"It was like I switched from a nightmare to the most fantastic dream I could ever have. You were in my bed and practically naked."

She smiles. "You actually *were* naked, which was a surprise. It was a good surprise but a surprise nonetheless."

"I think we need to even the score on that point."

I lean onto my side and pull Melanie's nightshirt over her head, revealing her perfectly round breasts. My mouth waters, and my body responds.

"Will, I'm glad you didn't leave. I was worried you would."

"I couldn't. I wanted you too badly. I have to warn you though, that small taste wasn't enough. It was too fast. I'm going to make love to you again, Melanie, and I'm going to take my time."

❖ ❖ ❖

This is too much. Too much emotion. Too much feeling. Too much dependence on this woman whom I know I shouldn't get too close to but can't stay away from.

Melanie smiles at me and hands me a cup of coffee. I hug her to me and kiss her temple.

I've fallen for her.

Hard.

And it isn't just the mind-blowing sex.

It's everything about her. She's smart, funny, beautiful, and loving. Being with her makes everything feel more intense. Still, nothing about my health has changed. I'm still broken from my experience on that street in Tikrit. There's no denying that. One night of insane sex isn't going to cure that. When I'm with Melanie, I feel bolstered, somehow more confident. That isn't reality. Geez. I need to think.

"I have to go."

Mel's smile falls. She doesn't look away. Instead, she keeps her eyes on me as if trying to read my thoughts.

"You're not running away, are you?"

"No." *Liar*.

"I'm not expecting anything from you that you can't give me. Last night was amazing. It was good for both of us." She places her hands on my chest. I feel their warmth through my sweater. "This doesn't have to be a one-time occurrence."

"You have Michael to take care of. I have myself

to take care of."

"Don't make excuses. Being with Michael is good for you. I can tell. And there are times when I'm home from work and Michael's in school. Those times can be good for you and me."

She makes a very good point. Maybe men do think with their other heads, because the thought of having a repeat of last night is enough to get me nodding my head in agreement.

"What do you have in mind?"

Her smile is back and bigger this time. Along with it is a brightness in her eyes.

"How about this?" She picks up a pumpkin from her countertop and steps toward the big picture window in her adjoining family room. "When the coast is clear, I'll put this pumpkin in this window like this." She places it on the window sill. "If you're feeling up to it, you can come over. If you have a headache or you're not feeling well, that's okay. I totally understand. We can make up for it the next time. What do you think about that?"

What do I think about that?

It's fantastic.

"I like it. When is Michael coming home today?"

"I'm picking him up in an hour. Then we're going to buy the rest of the items we need for his birthday party this afternoon."

"Right. Michael's party."

"It's just a small gathering with a few friends."

I walk into the family room to close the distance

between us. "Your pumpkin is in the window now."

"Yes, it is." She licks her lips and bites her lower lip.

My hands move to her waist, and I pull her to me. "You only have an hour to take a shower and get ready for your day." I reach between us and untie the knot on her robe. It falls to the sides to reveal the same nightshirt she wore briefly last night. "Let me help you get ready."

I take Mel's hand in mine and pull her with me back up the stairs. It was only twenty minutes ago that we dressed and came downstairs. We stop just inside her bedroom door. I slide my hands behind her neck and bring her lips to mine. She opens her mouth to me. My hands slide down her shoulders and arms, taking her robe off with them. Her fingers work the button on my jeans. We break our kiss long enough for my sweater and t-shirt to come over my head. Her nightshirt is next.

No panties. She didn't bother to put on her panties.

Heat flares through me again. I pick her up in my arms and carry her into the bathroom. The water warms while I taste each of her breasts in turn, teasing her nipples until she's panting for more.

We step into the warm shower. I place us such that my back takes the brunt of the water stream. Melanie's eyes are dark with desire. I want us to take our time. I lather my hands with soap and run them slowly down her back.

"Will," she whispers, the urgency clear.

"Not yet, sweetheart."

She wraps her hand around me. "Now, Will."

I cup her butt in my hands and lift her. Her legs wrap around me, and I give her exactly what she wants.

Chapter Twenty-One

Melanie

Hot.

My cheeks flush at the memory of my night with Will. There was a heck of a lot of heat in the shower this morning as well. A ragged sigh escapes me. I have to get myself together. Soon enough there will be nine boys and plenty of adults running around my yard.

We pull into our driveway at ten after noon. We have almost two hours to pull together the rest of the details for Michael's birthday party, which really is plenty of time if I can spend it working on party details and not daydreaming about my night with Will. All that's left is a little set-up, and Michael's excited to help with that. I had planned on finishing up most of these tasks last night after work. I'm not complaining though. My time was much better spent taking care of Will and then having Will take care of me.

Another pulse of heat flows through me. I have to get my head in the game.

"They're here!" Michael screams. Sure enough. The delivery truck from Bounce Mania pulls into the driveway behind me. I inhale deeply and slowly let it out. This is going to be a long day.

My phone chirps again. Since Will and I went our separate ways this morning, it's been one call or text after another with last-minute messages about the party.

"Sam's mom just texted me. He'll be able to make it after all." Michael squeals. That makes ten boys. What's one more, really?

We climb out of the car and introduce ourselves to Hank, the Bounce Mania delivery man. Michael points out the location where Hank should set up the Spiderman bounce house. I nod. I decided after much debate to just go ahead and hold Michael's party in the front yard. It's bigger and flatter than the back yard, and maybe that means fewer people traipsing through the house.

Michael carries the shopping bags with last-minute chips, and I carry the cake made by Mom's friend, Mrs. Mitchell. This one is yet another masterpiece. Mrs. Mitchell bakes just for fun in her retirement and does such an incredible job. The sheet cake depicts a city-scape. Spiderman is right in the middle, suspended by a frosting web from the top of the tallest building. Michael is thrilled with it, although he's already mentioned he wants to have a football party next year for his sixth birthday.

By two o'clock everything is ready to go for the party. We set up three long tables along the front of the house. The cake rests in the center of one with chips, candy, and fruit displayed around it. The other two tables hold jars of paint and small pumpkins for the boys to decorate. With all the excitement over the huge blow-up Spiderman bounce house, the kids may never want to decorate the pumpkins. Michael and his friends had jumped right inside, literally, and began going to town.

It's a perfect fall afternoon. The sun is warm, but the air is somehow crisp at the same time. I thank Mother Nature one more time for the beautiful weather, a very important unknown in the planning of this party.

The few school parents who stayed at the party stand together in a group talking. Mom, Dad, Hunter, Kate, Granny, and her boyfriend, Frank, sit together in a circle chatting with Will and me.

"Your eye looks much better, Granny. Are you worried about going back to bingo tonight?"

Mom sneers at my question and raises her chin slightly. Most people love Granny Simms to death. My mother isn't one of those people. Mom likes things to be just so. She doesn't care for people who rock the boat. Granny's habit of saying what's on her mind gives my mom the heebie-jeebies.

"You bet your sweet tookus I am." Frank and Hunter both wince. "I hope I win a game, too. I'll show that Gertie Cooper and everyone else. It takes a lot more than a jealous biddy and a black eye to stop me."

"Granny, you promised me you wouldn't get into another fight."

"I'm not going to start anything." She holds her chin a little higher. "You act like this escapade was my fault. It wasn't, you know. I was just defending myself. It was Gertie's fault. That woman should be in jail."

Kate and I share a knowing look. I can't hide my smile. Hunter shakes his head but doesn't respond. He has his work cut out for him.

I turn my gaze to Will, who's also smiling at Granny's situation. Something about his look becomes more personal, more knowing, like his smile is meant only for me. The green flecks in his brown eyes brighten. Man, Will's good looking. His chest is hard and muscular, and it feels...Snap out of it. I can't have these images going through my head right now.

I swallow hard. Kate giggles.

This is so embarrassing. I stand quickly. "I'll be right back. I forgot the cake server."

"I'll help you find it." Kate stands. "Plus, I have to go to the bathroom again. I'm barely pregnant, and I'm already going once an hour. I didn't think this would kick in for a while."

As soon as the front door is closed, Kate squeals and hugs me to her.

"I'm so happy for you. When did it happen?"

I can't help the grin that pops onto my face, but I still find it annoying that I'm so transparent. "What are you talking about?"

Kate holds me away from her and smirks. "Give me a break. You know exactly what I mean. You and Mr. Hot Stuff getting it on. I'm so happy for you."

"Last night." I walk toward the kitchen, and Kate follows. "God, help me. I really like him, Kate."

"What's wrong with that? You deserve to find someone special."

"I just don't want to fall too fast. Look what happened with Malcolm. I was totally in love with him, and he was an asshole."

Kate's hands move to her hips. Her lips purse.

"Will isn't an asshole."

"I know that." I do. "He's going through some stuff right now, and he's been very clear with me that he doesn't want a relationship."

Kate shrugs. "Trust me, Will's completely into you. I've seen how he looks at you. Smoldering is the word that comes to mind."

Smoldering—that's how I feel when I'm anywhere near him.

"You go ahead back outside. I wasn't kidding about having to use the bathroom."

A huge smile spreads across my face. Kate's pregnant. I'm very much in *like.* Life is good. My smile lasts until I take one step back onto the porch, and then it completely falls away.

Malcolm.

He walks toward me with a wrapped gift in his hand.

My knees weaken.

Please don't let Michael see him.

My gaze moves to Will. He's spotted Malcolm, too. He stands and so does my father. Hunter as well. The group of men moves toward Malcolm. I reach him first.

"What are you doing here?"

"It's my son's birthday party."

"No, you need to leave."

Will reaches us now, his hands fisted at his sides. Malcolm is fit, but Will and Hunter both seem to tower over him.

"I want to celebrate my son's birthday. I'm not trying to start anything. I even paid to have the mulch put down to help make the party nicer."

"Why would you do that?"

"I just wanted to help. He's my son, too."

"Please leave." I hear the pleading of my own voice. I don't want to beg Malcolm, but I'll do anything to keep Michael from knowing who he really is.

"Melanie asked you to leave." Will speaks the words through clenched teeth. He takes a step closer to Malcolm.

Crap. I don't want Malcolm here, but more than that, I don't want a fight. This is Michael's birthday party. Some of the school parents are already watching us nervously. I don't want to be known as the family with *domestic issues.* Michael doesn't need that pressure.

Hunter comes to the rescue. "Malcolm, I'm Police Officer Hunter Simms. We met at Minnie's last week. I'm asking you to please leave this property."

Malcolm looks from Hunter to Will to me. "Fine. Please make sure Michael gets this." He hands the wrapped package to me, and I take it. I don't want it, but I want Malcolm out of here.

"Mommy." Michael tugs on my sweater. "Are you okay? Who is that?"

Dread fills me. This is my worst nightmare come to life. Okay, maybe not my *worst* nightmare but a nightmare nonetheless. Anxiety and worry fill Michael's eyes. His forehead is wrinkled.

"This is Malcolm. He's someone I used to know who came by to bring you a birthday present. He can't stay though."

I hold my breath and watch helplessly as Michael checks out his father. *Please, Malcolm, don't tell Michael.* Thank the heavens, he doesn't. "Nice to meet you, Michael," is all he says. Michael smiles tentatively and turns back to me.

"Can we have cake now?"

I take my first breath in what seems like an eternity. "Sure, pumpkin. Why don't you go gather up your friends?"

Michael runs back toward the bounce house. I don't even care that he didn't say thank you.

Malcolm sneers. He thinks he's won. Score a point for him, I guess. "Goodbye, Melanie. Goodbye Mr. and Mrs. Woodside."

I turn to see Mom standing beside me. She's the only one in our group who doesn't look disgusted. I lean into Will, and he puts his arm around me for support. Mom makes a face of disapproval. Right now, I couldn't care less. I concentrate on breathing. This was a close call, and as much as I'd like to shout and cry and eat an entire bag of potato chips, I can't do any of those things right now. I have to serve cake for my son's birthday party. I take one more deep breath, stand up straight, and do just that.

"Malcolm's coming here today should show you how serious he is about wanting you and Michael in his life again."

Mom speaks the words as if she's giving an announcement that's beyond reproach or argument.

"How can you say that? Malcolm knows I don't

want him here. I've asked him more than once to stay away from us."

"You're blowing this way out of proportion. Malcolm brought a gift to his son on his birthday, and he hired a lawn service to spruce up your yard for the party. He did nothing wrong, and yet that crazy person living next door looked like he was about to punch him."

"Will's not crazy. He's a military hero whom I like very much. He's a much better man than Malcolm will ever be. Why can't you see that?"

Mom scoffs. I look to Dad for help. *Nothing*. Dad turns and walks back toward the family room to hang out with Michael. I love my Dad, but he's spineless when it comes to Mom. Dad likes Will. I know he does. Why can't he help me out here? *Big sigh*. As usual, I'm on my own here.

"Mom, this makes no sense. How can you want me to be with the man who walked out on me when I was pregnant? Even if I did love Malcolm—and I don't, mind you—what would stop him from leaving us again? You should be like Grace Richardson and hate his guts because of what he did to me."

Big mistake. I know it as soon as the words are spoken. Mom purses her lips and looks away. "Grace Richardson. *Ha*. What does she know? She'd rather you and Michael be alone than be a family? Michael needs his father."

"Michael needs *a* father, but it doesn't have to be Malcolm."

A vision of Will and Michael playing in the leaves pops into my head. It's too soon for these kinds of thoughts. I push it away, but it's only replaced with others. Will carrying Michael to his bedroom. Will sitting on the couch explaining each play of the football game. I swallow hard. Geez, I do have it bad, and so does my son. We're both in love with Will.

"I'm the first to admit that Malcolm treated you abominably. Trust me, I don't think you should just take him back with open arms. Make him work for it, sure. But, take him back. He loves you."

"He doesn't love me or Michael."

"Of course he does. Why else do you think he would come here?"

"I have no idea."

Chapter Twenty-Two

Will

"I heard what happened yesterday at Michael's party."

These are Aunt Bunny's first words to me when I walk into her room Sunday morning. I'd waited until my usual morning visitation time to give Aunt Bunny the news about Malcolm showing up at Michael's birthday party. I shouldn't be surprised that Granny, and who knows who else, beat me to it.

"Of course you did."

She shrugs. "News travels fast in Davidson."

I take a seat in the chair next to hers. She looks good today. Her cheeks have color, and her light blue eyes are bright.

"How are you feeling?"

"I feel really good today. Don't change the subject." Bunny leans toward me and places her hand on my knee. "I'm glad you were there for Melanie. You stood up to Malcolm, and he left."

"It was all I could do not to hit him. That would have been a disaster. He was just standing there with this entitled attitude. He's a complete asshole."

"He is, no doubt about that. You stood up to him though, and he backed down. Maybe that's what he needed to get the hint. Maybe now that he knows you're here, Malcolm will leave Melanie and Michael alone."

"No chance. You could see it in his eyes. Sure, Malcolm didn't spill the beans to Michael about being his father, but Michael knows he exists. Malcolm views that as a small victory, I'm sure. I wish I knew what he was up to. I don't buy his repentant father routine. He's up to something."

"How is Melanie?"

"I don't know."

"Why not? You weren't with her last night?"

I shake my head. "Her parents were there until late. I thought it might be a good idea to give her some space."

Aunt Bunny narrows her eyes and tilts her head. It feels like she's looking down on me, even though I have several inches on her.

"You mean give yourself some space. Some time to reflect on what is happening between you. Just don't hide from Melanie. You two are good for each other."

"How do you know that? You're in this place."

"I broke my hip, not my eyes. You and Melanie have both changed since finding each other."

"How have I changed?"

"Your looks are less severe. You're sleeping better and having fewer headaches. You smile more, especially when you speak of Melanie or Michael. You know it's true. Why do you keep trying to run away from it?"

Big sigh. It is true. I've noticed an improvement, but I still have so far to go.

"Having a couple headache-free days doesn't mean I'm cured. I'm still a mess. Not only will I likely never be a Marine again, but I also can't reliably do anything. It could take years before I'm able to hold down a job. Melanie doesn't need that kind of failure in her life."

Aunt Bunny takes my hand in hers. "No one is expecting you to run out and get a job. Melanie already has one."

"So, I'm supposed to move in with them and let Melanie provide for me. I don't think so."

"Don't be stupid. There are lots of ways to provide. They don't all require a nine-to-five job. Besides helping out around the house, there are jobs you could do at home. You write in those notebooks all the time. You could write a best-selling thriller about your experience or a book to help others with

PTSD, people who are going through the same thing you are. I know you're a good writer. You won that writing contest in high school. "

"Let me get this straight, you're saying I should be a house husband or write self-help books?"

"If that's what makes you and Melanie happy, I see nothing wrong with any of it. There are plenty of jobs you can do at home."

Another sigh. If it were anyone other than Aunt Bunny giving me this advice, I'd already have walked out. "I can't drag Melanie down with me. You have to understand that."

"What if you both pull each other up? Think about that."

The chime of the doorbell is a welcome sound. Whoever is at the door will be a distraction from the thoughts racing through my head, and God knows I need a break. I open the door to a smiling Michael. He holds the football I gave him for his birthday.

"Wanna play catch?"

"I'd love to, but with a football, we don't say *play catch*. We say *practice passing* or *throw the ball around*."

"Yeah. Let's do that."

I can't help but return Michael's enormous grin. My sneakers sit next to the door. I slip them on and join Michael outside. It's another sunny day, even warmer than yesterday.

Melanie sits on their front steps. She smiles at me, and I'm warmed even more. She stands when we get closer. I search her expression for anger or disappointment, any sign that she was displeased with my actions yesterday at Michael's party. I see nothing unhappy. She looks perfectly lovely. She's dressed in jeans and a pink t-shirt. Her brown hair is back in a ponytail. She looks relaxed and happy.

"I'm glad you're up for this. Michael doesn't want to throw with me."

"Are you kidding? I wouldn't miss it."

Michael looks up at me with the same excited grin on his face. "Let's start with how to hold the football." I demonstrate the proper hold myself and then place the ball properly into Michael's hand. I had bought a smaller, youth ball in the hopes that it would fit into Michael's hand, and it does. "How does that feel?"

He shrugs. "Okay."

"Now, when you throw it, you make a motion like this?" I demonstrate the action and the follow through. Michael copies my motions, letting the ball go. It sails through the air easily. "That's exactly how you do it."

Michael retrieves the ball, and we continue to throw it back and forth. I give him tips here and there where needed, but the kid has some talent.

Melanie watches us, giving Michael words of encouragement from time to time. She gives me plenty of smiles.

Maybe Bunny is right. Maybe somehow I can figure out a way to stay here in Davidson with Melanie and Michael. Am I selfish for wanting more perfect moments like this?

Mel answers her back door with a huge smile on her face. I return it with a tentative one of my own and step inside her kitchen. She closes the door behind me.

"I wasn't sure you'd actually go through with the pumpkin thing."

This sentence doesn't convey what I'm really thinking, which is more like *I've been hoping and watching to see that pumpkin show up in your window*. Melanie leans forward and wraps her arms around my neck. My arms slide around her waist.

"Why wouldn't I?" She kisses me lightly on the cheek. "I've been counting the minutes until I dropped Michael off at school this morning."

I brush my fingertips lightly against her cheek. "Do we need to talk about what occurred at Michael's party? We haven't had a chance to discuss it, and I want to be sure you're okay with what happened. I came really close to punching Malcolm."

"You stood up for me. I appreciate that, and you didn't hit him."

"But I wanted to."

"So did I. I wanted to punch him again Saturday night and then again on Sunday when Michael asked me questions about him. I appreciate that Malcolm didn't tell Michael who he really is, but Michael knows that something's going on. Children have a sixth sense about things they're not supposed to know."

"There's something else I did that you might not like."

"If you're talking about the fact that you cleaned out my gutters, I'm torn. You don't need to keep doing my household projects, but I'm glad the job's done."

"Not that." Her eyes narrow. "I asked Hunter about the possibility of getting a restraining order."

Melanie's mouth opens in surprise. "What did he say?"

"That it isn't an option at this point. Malcolm hasn't made any threats against you. He's been by to visit you here and at work, but he hasn't trespassed."

Melanie lets out a deep sigh. "Malcolm wanted nothing to do with Michael when we got the divorce. He gave up all rights to him. Why is he back now?" I shrug my shoulders. "Do you think he'll take me back to court?"

"I don't know. He might try, but he hasn't paid any child support or tried to see Michael for five years. There can be no good to come from him showing up now."

Melanie frowns and looks away. Why did I bring

this up? I guess I had to, but Melanie was smiling when I got here. Now, she's biting her lower lip—her tell that she's worried.

"Hunter and I talked about something else, too."

"What?"

"A double date. What do you think of getting a babysitter for Michael?" Melanie's eyes meet mine. "I've never been to Mayfair, but Hunter says it's a nice place. We were thinking we could go tomorrow."

"I would love to."

Melanie brings her lips to mine. Our soft kiss deepens. She squeals when I pick her up and begin walking toward the stairs.

I love pumpkins.

Chapter Twenty-Three

Melanie

"I can't thank you enough for watching Michael tonight."

Grace waves me off. "Sweetheart, I'm thrilled to do it. I love Michael to death, and besides that, it gives me practice for when I become a grandmother. You are going to knock that man's socks off when he sees you in that dress."

That's the plan. Even though I spent two hours getting ready and I've already slept with Will, I'm a nervous wreck. It's more than just the fact that I haven't been on a date since Malcolm. I'm in serious danger of getting my heart smashed into bits.

Will has made it clear to me from the beginning

that he isn't looking for a relationship. He's leaving town in a couple weeks. Neither of those things have stopped me from falling head over heels in love with him. When I'm with Will, I'm happier than I've ever been.

My mother, however, is not happy. She refused to watch Michael this evening if it meant I could go to dinner with *that man*. Honestly, she's living in some false reality where Malcolm isn't the bad guy. Malcolm will never be a father to Michael. He had his chance for that.

Will, on the other hand, would make an excellent father.

I push that thought out of my head. Of course, this isn't the first time I've had the thought. Visions of Will playing in the leaves with Michael and teaching him how to throw a football often pop into my mind. They're quickly followed up with Will's words that he can't be a permanent part of our lives. Maybe Will should open his eyes and see how good we all are for each other.

"You okay, Mel?"

I start as if awakened from a dream. "I'm sorry. I guess I was lost in thought."

The musical sound of the doorbell rings through the air and saves me from further discussion. Michael runs to the front door. The two of us had a talk earlier today about me dating Will. Michael loved the idea. Michael loves Will, just like I do. If I had been smart, I would have kept us at a distance, but in truth, I think Michael fell in love with him before I did.

Will wears charcoal dress pants and a white dress shirt. No tie, but he doesn't need one for tonight. Mayfair isn't that fancy.

I feel the heat of Will's gaze as he checks out my dress. I was hoping for this reaction. Kate insisted everyone needs a little black dress and wouldn't relent until I bought it. I thought it was a stupid purchase at the time because I felt I was someone who would never have an occasion to wear it. Thank goodness I was wrong.

Michael hugs both Will and me goodbye. "I'll be back soon, sweetheart. You be good for Miss Grace."

"Okay, Mommy." One more tight hug, and he practically pushes us out the door.

"Some kids wouldn't like their mothers going out on a date. It's a good thing Michael likes me."

"Michael loves you."

Was that too much? Maybe. It's the truth. It's not like I said *I'm in love with you*. He doesn't need to know that yet. Will's expression becomes thoughtful. I take his hand and let him pull me toward his car.

"Brady is one of the owners of the restaurant we're visiting tonight. Did you know that?"

"Yeah. He talked about it some when we were out fishing the other day. He seems like a good guy. It'll be nice to see him again."

"His partner and the chef is Meg McMann. Have you met her yet?"

"No. I've heard the name."

"She just married Tyler, one of the policemen who works with Hunter. You met him at Minnie's last week."

"Right."

The trip to Mayfair is a short one, only a few minutes. It's located in the heart of the downtown area, diagonally across the street from the General Store. Since all the other businesses are closed in the evenings, we find parking near the entrance. That's a good thing for me. These heels are the highest I own.

"Hold tight. I'll get your door."

Will does just that. I take his arm, and we walk into Mayfair together.

Downtown Davidson is the area where Main Street and Cherry Street intersect. The buildings on these blocks are all similar. Some have more flair than others, but they are all two stories tall. Unlike the general store across the street that has taken over the surrounding storefronts, Mayfair is housed in only the original corner spot. It's quaint, but lovely. The floors are also original. They're polished oak and glimmer when the light hits them just right. The small space only allows room for about fifteen or so small tables, which are covered with white cloths and usually hold candles and small flower arrangements.

Mayfair has only been open since May. In those five months, Brady and Meg have turned it into a gastronomic experience. We used to have to drive to

Charlottesville to have dinner at a fancy restaurant. Now, people from Charlottesville drive here, to Davidson.

"Good evening." Brady meets us at the door. The formality ends there. Brady pulls me in for a hello hug. Will gets an enthusiastic handshake. "Hunter and Kate just arrived. I'll show you to them."

We follow Brady toward the back where I see my friends waiting for us. Kate gives me a wave, which I return. Will places his hand on the small of my back. It's not like I need the help to navigate through the tables, but I like feeling the pressure of his hand there.

Hunter and Kate stand when we arrive at the table. We hug hello and take our seats across from them. Brady introduces us to Helen, our waitress. I don't know her, but I've seen her here before. She's forty or so. She wears the same black slacks and white tuxedo-type shirt as the other servers. Her long hair is pulled back in a bun. There's something very sweet and affable in her appearance that goes beyond being polite to us as customers. She seems genuinely friendly and happy to be here.

Kate and I typically order cocktails during the rare times we get out for dinner. Not tonight, and not for the next nine months, at least. In solidarity, I order a club soda with lime. Will does the same. He takes my hand under the table. Our fingers entwine together naturally. Being with Will feels natural. This evening feels natural. Does Will think so as well? Is there a chance he might stay in town longer to see where this goes? What's the hurry with him leaving? I'm sure Bunny would love to have Will here.

"What are you going to order? I can't decide between the braised pork chop and the filet—definitely feeling like something hearty though."

Busted. While I've been staring at the menu, I haven't seen a word of it. I've been caught up in my thoughts about Will.

"I'm not sure yet," I answer quickly. "Both of those sound really good. You can't go wrong with anything Meg makes."

"Glad to hear that." The words come from behind me. I turn to see Meg wearing her chef coat and a huge smile.

I introduce her to Will. She says quick hellos to everyone at the table before ducking back into the kitchen. This is how it usually works when we come here for dinner. We sit close to the kitchen, and Meg sneaks out to see us when she can get away. We've joked about putting a table in the kitchen, but there's no room for that.

Helen returns to take our dinner orders. I go with the field greens salad and the monkfish. Truthfully, I'm starving. Being with Will during the day is tiring. Not that I'm in any way complaining. It's quite wonderful, actually. It's only been two days, but I like the pattern that seems to be emerging. We make love and then talk. We make love again and then nap together. My nap is much shorter than

Will's. I get up after an hour or so and do some things around the house that need to get done. I wake Will before I leave to pick up Michael from school. Will sleeps restfully during that time, so I let him sleep. No screaming or thrashing about. It may be my imagination, but Will seems better rested now that we're together. The puffiness around his eyes has diminished. Maybe that's just wishful thinking.

"I feel a bit at a loss here. The three of you have known each other practically your whole lives."

"I can't imagine what it would be like to have a life of moving from place to place," Hunter replies. "I've lived in the same house since I was eight. There are other places I'd like to see, but Davidson will always be home."

He and Kate share a knowing look. It's hard to believe they had so many years where they didn't get along. They're certainly making up for it now.

Chapter Twenty-Four

Will

The air in here suddenly feels thick and muggy. I swallow hard and turn my head to look away from Hunter and Kate. They're not doing anything other than staring at each other, and yet it feels like we're intruding on their private moment.

Melanie gives me a small smile. She feels it, too. I tighten my grip on her fingers and watch as her smile grows. Being here tonight feels so right, just like almost every moment I've had with Melanie since I met her. Sure, we had a rocky start, but nothing feels rocky about our relationship now.

Relationship.

Did I really just have that thought? The fact that I'm a mess hasn't changed. I can't deny, however, that I feel like less of a mess when I'm with Melanie. Michael, too. I feel like I belong here.

Can I do this?

Maybe.

I take a deep breath and let it out slowly. On the outside, I force myself to remain quiet. On the inside, I feel like I've made a huge step forward. Maybe it wouldn't hurt to give things with Melanie a shot. I don't mean propose or move in. I mean only to stay in town a while longer to see where this path takes us.

"How is Bunny feeling?" I look up to see Hunter waiting for an answer. "Granny says she seems to be doing a lot better."

"She is. I spoke with her doctor this afternoon. It looks like she might be coming home soon. She might even get to come home on Friday."

"Really?" Melanie's eyes widen in surprise. "It's just that you didn't say anything. We need to have a welcome home party for her."

"That's a great idea," Kate chimes in. "Nothing huge that would wear her out, but poor Bunny's been in that rehab place much too long. I'll make a couple pans of lasagna, and we can get Granny to make her chocolate cake."

"If things are slow, I can probably get out of work early. Michael will be thrilled."

I've known my whole life that Aunt Bunny is a

special person. Seeing how much her friends love her makes me swell with pride. My parents and I have both worried about her being alone here since Uncle Jimmy passed away. She isn't alone at all, though. It's like she has another family.

"I'm sure Aunt Bunny would love a party. I know she can't wait to come home."

Our server places our dinners in front of us. My short ribs look incredible.

I lean close to Melanie and whisper in her ear. "Sorry I didn't tell you about Bunny coming home on Friday. I meant to, but you look so beautiful in this dress that I forgot everything else."

Melanie smiles, and I know I'm forgiven.

"Back to your usual visiting time, I see."

Bunny seems extra chipper this morning. She's dressed up again—a look I truly appreciate on her. It's easy to deduce that sweatpants equal a painful day for her.

"I don't think I've been in town long enough to have a *usual visiting time*."

She tilts her head forward giving the effect of rolling her eyes. "You do, actually. The last two days you didn't get here until after three o'clock. Dare I say about the time Melanie leaves to pick up Michael from school?"

I'm a grown man who's fought for my country

and seen much of this world. Why does this conversation somehow make me feel like a teenager who's been sneaking out to visit his girlfriend?

A small sigh escapes. "That's a coincidence. I'm here now."

A grin forms that spans her entire face. "Don't you lie to me, young man. You're here because Melanie is working today. You were late on the days that she has off. I wasn't born yesterday, and none of that matters anyway. I'm so thrilled for both of you. You deserve some love in your life."

"Fine. I do like Melanie." The words are out. Despite my worries on the subject, it feels good to speak them out loud. "A lot."

"Of course you do. Fate works in mysterious ways."

Wait a minute. Aunt Bunny seems a little too happy with herself. "Maybe in this case, fate had a little help?"

She shrugs. "I don't see anything wrong with guiding fate a little bit. We all have our part in God's big plan. I admit it. I was hoping you two would hit it off. The important thing to me is that you're happy, and so is Melanie. You both deserve some happiness in your lives."

I shake my head mostly at myself, surprised that I hadn't thought of this before. Bunny invited me up here to Davidson for a reason. It just wasn't the reason I thought.

"I appreciate your efforts in matchmaking and

all, but I'll be going home soon."

Aunt Bunny's blue eyes widen. Her mouth opens in surprise. "Why?"

"Dr. Hopkins is releasing you tomorrow. You're getting along fine. You don't need me here to take care of you."

Aunt Bunny pats my knee. "I didn't ask you to visit because I needed to be taken care of. I like having you here, and you like being here. You have no reason to go back to Florida."

"I do. I live there. I have to get my life back together and figure out my next move."

"Nonsense. Your life is here now."

"Where am I supposed to live?"

"I'm not asking you to make any big life-long plans. You can stay with me for now. My house is plenty big enough for both of us."

Could I really stay here in Davidson?

Maybe. The thought of going back to Florida to that sterile apartment I call home sure doesn't feel right. Melanie's house has pumpkins, Michael's toys here and there, chores that need to be done. Michael needs someone to throw the football with. Aunt Bunny's right, of course. Is she ever wrong about anything?

Chapter Twenty-Five

Melanie

"Geez, Melanie, could you be more of a drama queen?"

I look up from my seat at the nurse's station to find Ellen standing over me. I was so engrossed in reviewing the notes and test results for little Timmy O'Reilly in room four that I didn't notice Ellen was so close. Her blue eyes flash annoyance as I struggle to remember what it was that she'd just said.

Wait. What? Me, a drama queen?

I square my shoulders and keep my gaze locked with hers. "No one has ever called me that before."

Ellen shrugs. "That's what you sound like to me. A restraining order? Really?"

"I don't know how you heard about that, but not only is it none of your business, I couldn't get one."

"Exactly. You couldn't get one because Malcolm hasn't done anything other than try to have a relationship with his son. That isn't a crime. It shows what a good person he is. And he's with me now. You can't have him back."

Is she kidding? The heat burns in the pit of my stomach. I'm not sure where all this is coming from. Ellen's always seemed like a perfectly reasonable person. We've never been close, but I thought she respected me professionally. I tried to warn her about getting involved with Malcolm. She obviously didn't listen. Maybe I should warn her more strongly? There's probably no point in that. I've done what I can, and she hasn't listened to a word I said.

"The situation between Malcolm and me is none of your business. If you're smart, you'll stay away from him. You need to trust me."

Yeah. I couldn't let it go without some kind of warning. I know as soon as the words leave my mouth that I went about it all wrong. I just kind of blurted them out. Not a good plan.

Ellen scoffs.

"Malcolm's coming here today to meet me for lunch. Just wanted to let you know."

What did I ever do to her?

The rest of Friday is too busy to worry about Ellen. The spare time I have to think about personal topics is spent much more pleasantly with thoughts of Michael and Will. There are a couple thoughts of Bunny that sneak in as well. Mostly those considerations are along the lines of me worrying about getting to her welcome home party before it ends.

I arrive at Bunny's at seven-thirty, which is about the time I would get home on a normal work day, but an hour and a half late for the party. Luckily, I was able to steal a few quick moments to change clothes before I left the hospital, and I'm glad I did. I park in my driveway and walk straight over to Bunny's house.

The welcome home banner Michael decorated hangs above the steps. I helped him with the spacing, but he did the writing and all the coloring on the four-foot banner himself. He wanted to be sure it was the first thing Bunny saw when she came home.

Bunny herself answers the door. Her smile is bright as she pulls me into a tight embrace. "Melanie, honey, we've been waiting for you." When she pulls back, I see that her eyes are wet with tears. She gives me one more quick embrace before turning and heading toward her dining room.

Bunny's house is bigger than mine. She has a formal living room and dining room at the front of the house that I don't have. Will turns the corner from the kitchen and plants a quick kiss on my cheek. Warm thoughts flow straight to my core. What a wonderful feeling to be welcomed home like this.

"You're just in time for dinner."

My warm thoughts are replaced with a jolt of panic.

"You haven't eaten yet? I asked you to start without me. I didn't want to hold up dinner for everyone."

"We all wanted to wait. It's not a party without you." *Kate*. She gives me a hello hug. Now this really feels wonderful. This is supposed to be Bunny's welcome home party, but I feel like it was meant for me.

The next few minutes are a blur as we exchange greetings and take a seat at Bunny's large dining room table. It is set with a beautiful tablecloth, three small flower arrangements, and place cards. Two large pans of lasagna sit between the flower arrangements within easy reach of everyone at the table. We each have a salad plate already loaded with salad. I know Kate is responsible for the set-up. She's really good at entertaining, and her style shows.

Bunny sits at the head of the table. Will sits next to her, then Michael and me. Michael insisted he be allowed to sit between us. Granny is next to me, and her boyfriend, Frank, sits at the other end of the table. Hunter sits next to him, and then Kate and her parents. My own parents were invited but made an excuse. I'm not surprised. They've never been close with Bunny, and I know they feel even more uncomfortable now that I'm with Will. Mom only sighed when I asked her to drop Michael off at Bunny's house at five-thirty. I'm sure Mom wasn't rude, but I sure hope she was cordial.

"This dinner looks amazing, Kate. I can't thank you all enough for this fabulous welcome home." It hits me then that I did nothing to help out with this event. As if Bunny can read my mind, she says, "Thanks especially to Melanie."

"But I didn't do any of this."

Bunny smiles. "You, my dear, are responsible for the most important thing of all." I rack my brain, trying to figure out what she could be talking about. "You brought my Will back from the depths of depression. That's the best gift anyone could have given me."

The heat flares on my cheeks. I sneak a look at Will. Hints of pink dot his cheeks, but he's smiling. He raises his glass. "To Melanie." Everyone at the table lifts their glasses and repeats Will's words. I see their movements out of the corner of my eye, but I don't take my eyes off of Will and his smile.

Michael pulls his knees up into the chair and rests on them so he can reach me for a kiss. While part of me would like this perfect moment to go on forever, I need to get the attention off of me. I swallow down the knot of emotion so that I can speak.

"I think we should be toasting Bunny. She's the one who's healthy and home at last."

"Hear, hear," says Mr. Richardson.

I raise my glass and take in a healthy and glowing Bunny. "To Bunny." My words are repeated, and we take another drink.

"I'm thrilled to make it home in time for Halloween. I can't wait to see all the trick-or-treaters. It's one of my favorite nights of the year."

"So much so that she made me stop at the General Store to get candy on the way home this afternoon." We all share a laugh.

"What are you dressing up as, Michael?"

"Spiderman." Michael practically shouts the word. He is very excited about Halloween this year. "I have a mask and everything."

"I can't wait to see it."

"Halloween has never been so great for us. Living out in the country, we don't get any trick-or-treaters. They all come into town so they don't have to walk so far between the houses. Hunter, can we stop by here on our way to bingo tomorrow? I would love to see Michael in his costume."

"Sure, Granny."

"They're still going to have bingo on Halloween?" Grace has been kind of quiet this evening.

"Bingo is the best on Halloween. We dress up, and they give out prizes like free bingo cards for the best costume."

"What are you going to be?" Michael asks.

"A boxer."

It's all I can do not to spit out the mouthful of wine I just drank. Granny's eye is still slightly bruised from the incident a couple weeks ago. Hunter and Frank both look uncomfortable. Poor Hunter. I know he loves Granny. Most grandsons wouldn't forego Saturday night plans to take their grandmother to bingo. She truly is a handful. If I were as close as he is to the situation, I might not think Granny is such a hoot, but how can I not?

"What's your costume like? Do you have boxing gloves?"

"Of course I have gloves to wear. I borrowed them from May's grandson. I'll wear them some of the time, but I'm planning to hang them from a string around my neck when I'm playing. My friend Hazel made me a special pair of shorts and a robe. You can see them tomorrow."

I truly cannot wait for that.

Chapter Twenty-Six

Will

"Melanie mentioned last night that she has a toilet that won't stop running."

Aunt Bunny mentions this household chore completely out of the blue. We've been sitting at her small kitchen table drinking coffee and reading the newspaper. Who knows where she's going with this. I just play along.

"Yeah, I need to take a look at that." Maybe later this afternoon if I can get this headache to go away. Maybe the excitement of Bunny coming home yesterday was too much. Maybe it was the fact that I couldn't get the look on Melanie's face when Bunny mentioned her saving me out of my mind. Whatever it was, I'd had a horrible night's sleep that left a nagging headache this morning.

"I'm sure that needs to get done right away. I was thinking that maybe I could hang out with Michael over here while you check out the toilet. It might take a few hours to get the job done, don't you think?"

A few hours? What?

Oh, so that's it.

I feel the tips of my mouth curve upward despite the fact that I'm shaking my head at Aunt Bunny's interference.

"Is this your way to get me to spend some alone time with Melanie?"

She smiles guiltily and shrugs her shoulders. "I don't know what you mean." Yeah, right. "I just want to make sure you have plenty of uninterrupted time to get the job done." *Get the job done.* Really? "Why don't you give Melanie a call and see what time works for her?"

I pick up my cell phone and send Melanie a text. She replies right away.

"Melanie will bring Michael over here at ten o'clock. Does that work for you?"

"It sure does. Don't even think of picking him up before two. We have a lot to do."

Melanie brings Michael over at ten o'clock on the

dot. He runs inside, thrilled at the idea of spending time with Bunny. She dismisses us with a quick goodbye and a wink. I intertwine my fingers with Melanie's and lead her back to her house.

The sky is dark and covered with a thick layer of clouds. They're predicting a few showers for today as a cold front pushes through the area. The rain should clear up in time for trick-or-treating, but the temperature will drop down into the twenties tonight.

Melanie stops walking and stares at her front door. I watch her in silence as she studies it.

"Do you not like the work the painters did? I think it looks pretty good."

Her nose wrinkles as obvious confusion sets in. "Did you do this, or was it Malcolm?"

"What?"

"The painting. Did you do it?"

"No. A man wearing painter's overalls was here yesterday for a couple hours. He painted the trim by the front door and the area around the patio in the back. I had nothing to do with it." I reach out and squeeze Melanie's forearm to keep her upright. She looks a little queasy. "Maybe it wasn't Malcolm. Maybe your father set it up. He seems like the kind of dad who would take care of his daughter."

"Hopefully. I really don't want it to have been Malcolm. Why would he pay someone to paint my house? The mulch was one thing, but this makes no sense."

"Do you want to call him? We can postpone this home improvement meeting until later if you want."

She smiles. "I'll talk to Dad later. I don't want to waste a minute of my time with you."

As soon as Melanie closes the door, I lean her against it and kiss her. She immediately opens her mouth to me. The feel of Mel's body pressed against mine causes a reaction. My body springs to attention. A moan escapes from the back of her throat. I'd gone months without being with a woman before I met Melanie. Now, it's only been three days since we've been together. Too long. I break our kiss and continue to stare into her eyes.

"It's kind of embarrassing that Bunny invited Michael over to her house. I mean, I'm very happy about it, but it's strange."

"I felt that way at first."

"And now?"

"I'm completely okay with it. If Bunny wants to give me the opportunity to be with you, there's no way I'm going to pass it up."

Mel's face falls. Her eyes have lost their shine. She looks away and focuses on something across the room. I cup her chin and turn her face back toward me.

"What's wrong?"

"You're going to be leaving soon. I know you warned me not to expect anything from you, and I don't. But, that doesn't mean I don't feel sad that you're leaving. I like spending time with you."

"I like spending time with you, too." Her eyes moisten. She keeps them focused on mine. "In fact, the more time I spend with you and Michael, the more impossible it seems for me to leave."

Melanie sucks in a startled breath and lets it out in a whoosh. A single tear falls down her cheek.

"Really? You're going to stay?"

"I'm going to try. My reasons for not having a relationship are still valid. I'm a mess. But, when I'm with you, I'm better. I haven't had any bad dreams when I've napped here at your house. I still have them when I sleep at Bunny's but not as often. My headaches aren't as bad either. That could be because I'm sleeping better overall, or it could be because my dreams are more pleasantly occupied with thoughts of you."

"Let's go make some more memories for you to dream about."

Melanie flattens her hands against my chest and pushes me away from her. She locks the door and walks toward the stairway. I follow. She looks back and smiles again before pulling her sweater over her head, revealing her firm back. My mouth goes dry. She drops the sweater on the floor and keeps walking. Her bra is next. That lands on the stairs.

She steps out of her shoes at the top of the staircase and continues down the hall. Her jeans land in the hallway outside her bedroom door. I turn into the room to find her lying on her bed completely naked. A shiver travels through me as I take in her absolute beauty. I want to kiss every inch of her and make her mine.

Chapter Twenty-Seven

Melanie

The look on Will's face says it all. *He wants me.* Malcolm never looked at me quite like that. Maybe that's because he didn't want me long term. Will said he didn't want me for the long term either, and yet, he's staying. It's funny how life works out differently than you think it will.

Will doesn't have as much fanfare with his undressing. His clothes are off in a matter of seconds. He crawls onto the bed and kisses the middle of my tummy. He trails kisses down my hip to my thigh. My body pulses, waiting and hoping that his journey is about to come to an end. He nudges my legs apart. A moan escapes me, and he continues his kisses right on target. My breathing turns to panting as I get closer and closer to the edge.

Just as I'm about to go over, he pulls away. I lean up on my elbows to see what on earth could have made him stop. He grins at me. I fall back to the bed and lift my hips, urging Will to continue. He does, but only for a few brief seconds. He stops again.

"What are you trying to do to me?"

"You'll see."

"I don't want to see. I want you inside me right now."

"Ooh. I like it when you're bossy."

"Will, I can't wait much longer."

"You won't have to, sweetheart."

Sweetheart. There's barely time for the name to register in my brain before he covers me. The feel of him inside me is enough to make me not only go over the edge, but shoot like a rocket into outer space. I cling to him and hold on tightly until he groans and falls on top of me.

We lay together catching our breath until he rolls off me. Will lays a protective arm over me and kisses the back of my head. Feeling overwhelmingly tired, I let sleep take me.

The jerk of Will's body wakes me from a sound sleep. He mumbles something I can't quite make out.

Uh oh.

He's having a bad dream at my house. I guess it was too much to hope that he never would. Will's forehead furrows. He shakes his head from side to side and kicks his leg out toward the side of the bed. Before I have time to get out of bed, his arm flails toward me. Will's hand connects directly with my eye. I scream out and then quickly snap my mouth shut.

Too late. My scream pulls Will from his dream. He sits up quickly and studies me with suddenly alert eyes.

"Shit. Melanie, no."

"I'm fine, Will. It was just an accident."

My eye feels like it's about to explode. It doesn't feel fine. I will my blood to not rush to the area and make a bruise. From the look on Will's face, I'm too late.

His hand reaches toward me. His fingers brush softly against my cheek.

"I'm so sorry."

He stands and dresses without looking at me. The whole time I'm trying to reassure him. I*t was an accident. I know you didn't mean to do this. It doesn't hurt much at all.*

"I knew you were having a bad dream. It's my own fault. I should have gotten out of bed."

"Don't *ever* say that again."

"Please don't leave. Stay here and talk to me about this."

Will gives me one last look, his eyes full of pain.

"I...I have to go."

I push the tears back and climb out of bed. I pull my panties on. Just great. A leisurely striptease seemed like a good idea earlier. Now, I have to walk through the house to find my clothes. Better get to it.

My reflection catches my eye as I walk past the dresser mirror. I gasp. It's no wonder Will is so upset about this. Dark purple circles my eye, and it's getting darker by the minute.

Shit. My eye is tender, no doubt, but it doesn't feel nearly as bad as it looks. Even if it did, it doesn't matter. Will was asleep when he did this.

It. Was. An. Accident.

With a big sigh, I head into the hallway to retrieve my jeans. I slip on each piece of clothing as I find it and head out my front door in time to see Will pulling his truck out of Bunny's garage. I pick up my pace and run to him. He doesn't stop. He's gone in seconds.

Tears are flowing in earnest now. There's no way I can stop them. I walk into Bunny's garage to knock on her kitchen door, but there's no need. She stands in the open doorway. Her expression takes on an air of understanding at seeing me.

"You poor dear. What happened?"

"It was an accident. Will had a bad dream. He jerked his arm, and it caught me in the eye. That's all that happened." She walks carefully down the steps to be level with me on the garage floor and brings me in for a tight embrace. I breathe in the scent of her grandmother-ness. She smells of body powder and chocolate chip cookies. "He told me this morning he was going to stay. Will he leave now? What did he say?"

"He didn't say anything. He knocked on the door, stepped inside without a word, grabbed his truck keys off the hook in the kitchen, and left."

"He can't leave. I love him."

"I know you do, sweetheart. He loves you, too, you know."

"Can you watch Michael a while longer?"

Bunny nods. "Of course, honey. Anything you need."

I give her a quick kiss on the cheek and head back to my house for my phone. Will doesn't answer my calls. When the third call goes to voicemail, I leave him a message. "I understand why you're upset. I do. You have to understand. I don't blame you for this. It was an accident. I know you would never hurt me on purpose. Please don't leave without talking to me. Please, Will."

I disconnect. Too much pleading? Not if it works. Not if it makes Will understand.

I grab my purse off the kitchen counter and head out the door to my car. I have to find Will.

Chapter Twenty-Eight

Will

The reality of my actions weigh heavily on my chest. I should have left town when I had the chance. I never should have come here in the first place. I shouldn't have gotten involved with Melanie. I'm such a selfish bastard. Bunny gave me hope that things could work out for me. Melanie did, too. I wanted so badly to believe them.

Maybe in another life, things could have worked. Not in this one. It's like I told them all along, I'm a broken man. I didn't want to pull Melanie down into this hole with me, and that's exactly what I ended up doing. Sure, I didn't just haul off and hit her. I would never hit a woman on purpose. The fault is still mine. I knew what I was capable of. I broke Aunt Bunny's lamp. That should have been enough of a warning to not allow myself to get so close to Melanie. I did to Melanie's face what I did to that lamp.

I should have been stronger.

A quick knock is the only warning I get before Hunter walks into the small interrogation room. He wasn't working today. Bryce was the only person here at the station when I arrived. I requested to speak with Hunter, and he came in to see me. I've dragged him away from who knows what plans because of my bullshit.

"I want to turn myself in."

His face steels into his cop expression as if to ready himself for whatever it is that I'm about to tell him.

"For what?"

"I hit Melanie in the face."

Hunter takes a seat across the table from me. He hits a button on a device in the middle of the table. He's recording me. "Tell me what happened."

I sigh. "Aunt Bunny invited Michael over this morning to help her bake cookies and get ready for Halloween. That's what she said, anyway. In reality, she just wanted to give Melanie and me some time together." Hunter nods his understanding. I continue. "Afterwards"—hopefully details aren't necessary here—"we fell asleep. I had a nightmare." I look away from Hunter. His eyes are too full of understanding and maybe something else. Pity? No thank you. This is not the time for that. "I sometimes get violent in my sleep. I flailed my arm and hit Melanie in the face."

"Will, that sounds like it was an accident."

I sigh again. "That's what Melanie said. Of course I didn't mean to hit her, but I knew better than to allow myself to sleep with her. I should have known it wasn't safe for her, and because of my stupidity, Melanie was hurt."

"What kind of injury does she have?"

"A black eye that I know of. She should be taken to the hospital to be checked out to know for sure. Her nose didn't look crooked, and it wasn't bleeding, so it likely isn't broken."

Hunter nods again. "Is Melanie going to press charges?"

"I don't know. She should throw the book at me. If she doesn't, then you should make charges anyway. I put her in harm's way."

"What happens if no one presses charges? Then what would you do?"

"Leave town."

"I see." Hunter brings his hand to his chin, clearly in thought. "I'm not going to press charges at this time. I need to conduct an investigation first—you know, talk with Melanie and Bunny to corroborate your story. In the meantime, I'll have to hold you here at the station."

My turn to nod. This is exactly what I deserve.

"So, just to be clear, you're okay with staying here in the jail cell while I ask my questions?"

"Of course. That's what I deserve."

"Okay. Follow me."

We both stand, and I follow Hunter through an office area. Bryce sits behind a desk and watches us silently walk by. We turn down a short hallway to the holding area. There are two small jail cells. Both are empty. Hunter motions me inside, and I walk in without a word. The metal door clangs closed behind me.

"I'll be back as soon as I can. Bryce is outside. You can yell to him if you need a bathroom visit. I'm also going to let you keep your phone, so if you need anything, you call me, okay?" I nod, too disgusted with myself to speak. "It's going to be okay, you know. Sometimes the worst parts in our lives come just before the best ones." Hunter turns on his heel and leaves me alone to wallow in my own self-pity.

I take in what could very well be my home for a while. It's what you'd expect a jail cell to look like. The only thing missing is a window—there's not even one with bars on it. There's a bed on one side of the room and a metal chair across from it. Both pieces of furniture are bolted to the floor. There's also a toilet that's sparkling clean.

I take a seat on the bed and rest my elbows on my knees. This. Sucks.

Chapter Twenty-Nine

Melanie

Where is he? I've been driving around Davidson for almost an hour with no luck. Davidson's a small town. Finding Will shouldn't be this difficult, but I don't see his car anywhere. I've zigzagged through the downtown streets and the surrounding neighborhoods. I've been by Minnie's Diner twice and driven back to my own house three times on the hope that Will would be waiting for me in my driveway. Bunny hasn't called me, so I know she hasn't heard from him.

Where could he be?

Maybe he's just driving around processing what happened. The pounding rain doesn't make for good driving. *Please let him be okay.* Maybe he'll come to his senses and realize this isn't a big deal. He would never hurt me on purpose.

I make the turn down Cherry. *Just one more time.* Probably. If I could just find Will, then I wouldn't have to…

There it is. My foot brakes too hard as I strain to study the black Toyota Tundra parked in an angled spot near the police station.

No.

He wouldn't, would he?

With shaky hands, I pull my car into the first empty space I come to. I turn off the ignition and immediately drop my keys on the floorboard. My hands fumble for the keys as I try to catch my breath.

What is Will doing at the police station?

Maybe he's actually somewhere else nearby, and this is just where he found a parking space. This is a downtown street. He could be anywhere along here.

But he's not. I know he's in there. With a deep breath, I steel my nerves, get out of my car, and cross the street toward the station.

My phone chirps with a call. Hunter's photo flashes on the display. It's not Will. I take another deep breath and answer.

"Hunter, do you know where Will is?"

"I do. Can you meet me at the store? I need to talk with you."

Reality crashes over me, leaving me dizzy. "Sure.

I'll be there in a minute."

I walk the short block to the Richardson's General Store. The rain has fewer people out on the street than usual, but the couple snuggled under an umbrella look me over good. I must be quite a sight. My eye is sore, and I know there's a dark bruise. Luckily, there's nothing serious with the injury. My eye is still open a little, and my eyesight isn't very blurry.

I pause at the store window and remember it was just last week that I stood in this very spot with Will. I appreciated the view of pumpkin heaven a lot more that day.

"Mel, come inside. You're getting soaked out there."

A sigh escapes me. Kate's right. It doesn't really matter. I lift my head and turn to see Kate standing in the doorway. Her jaw drops at the sight of my face. *Great.*

"It's not as bad as it looks."

Kate pulls me into an embrace. I let the tears come.

"Oh, sweetie. Let's get you inside."

She pulls away, guides me to the soda fountain, and sits me down on one of the stools. Another place with good memories of Will.

Hunter places a hand on my shoulder. He winces at the sight of my eye but doesn't comment.

"Tell us what happened."

I launch into my story. They both stand quietly

nearby while I explain everything. I can't let Hunter get the wrong idea.

"Yes, technically, Will gave me a black eye, but it wasn't his fault. He was sleeping and had no idea what he was doing. Did he tell you that?"

Hunter nods. "He did. Will's concerned that he put you in danger in the first place. He knows you won't press charges. He believes he committed a crime, so he turned himself in to us."

"Where's Will now?"

"He's at the station. I'm holding him there temporarily."

I jump off the stool and turn to face Hunter. My face flashes with heat. I don't know if I've ever been this angry.

"You put Will in jail? How could you?"

"I did it to protect both of you."

I shake my head. How could he? I haven't been on friendly terms with Hunter Simms for very long, but he's my best friend's husband. Shouldn't he be on my side in this? I sneak a glance at Kate. Her expression is unreadable. If she had my side, I'd know it.

"That's bullshit. I don't need protection from Will."

"I know that, but Will doesn't."

"What are you talking about?"

"Will wanted to be put in jail. He went in voluntarily. He told me that if I didn't hold him, he'd leave town. As long as Will's locked in our little jail, he won't leave Davidson and mess up his chance at happiness with you."

The realization of what's happening sinks slowly through my indignation. Hunter is on my side. He's looking out for Will as well.

"Are you going to charge him with a crime?"

"Of course not. What would I charge him with? You both gave me the same story, and you don't want to press charges. There's nothing left to do."

"What happens now?"

Hunter sighs. "Now, let's give Will some time to think about what life will be like without you. If he doesn't come up with the correct solution on his own, then I'll do my best to talk some sense into him."

"Thank you, Hunter. I'm sorry I doubted you."

"I get it. You need to understand, though, I can't keep Will locked in that cell indefinitely. If he wants out, then I have to let him go."

"Should I go talk to him?"

"No," Kate answers firmly. "It'll be much better if Will decides to stay on his own. Know this, even if he does leave town right now, it won't be long until he realizes what he's missing and comes running back to Davidson. He loves both you and Michael."

"I know. He just told me this morning that he was going to stay and give us a chance. Michael will be devastated if he leaves, and so will I. It was all I could do to survive Malcolm leaving us. I can't handle it again."

"Isn't it strange how life works out?" Hunter and I both look at Kate. "Malcolm left because he thought he had to protect himself from you. Will wants to leave because he thinks he needs to protect you from himself. This is messed up."

No kidding.

It's going on five o'clock, and I'm a complete nervous wreck. I've received four texts from Hunter. None of them were particularly good. Leaving Will alone with his thoughts didn't bring the outcome I was hoping for—at least not yet. The later it gets, the more afraid I am that Will really is going to leave town. What if Kate's wrong? What if Will leaves Davidson and doesn't come back? Then what do I do?

The chime of the doorbell brings Michael screaming into the room from the kitchen. It's still daylight outside—too early for trick-or-treaters. My stomach somersaults at the hope that it might be Will. Surely Hunter would have told me if Will had left the station.

It isn't Will.

Granny and Kate stand just outside the door. Michael lets out an appreciative whoop when he sees Granny's costume. Even in my thoughtful fog, I can't miss it. She wears a bright red satin robe with white trim. The robe hangs open to reveal a white tank top and yes, hot pink boxing shorts. The shorts are long, ending just before her knees. Granny makes a motion with her hands as if she's pounding on someone with the boxing gloves she's sporting on each hand. The best part of Granny's costume is that she's carrying her purse in the crook of her arm, where she always carries it. What a sight.

"You look great, Granny." Michael beams. I can't help but smile my first smile all day. No. That's not true. There were lots of smiles this morning before... *it* happened. My smile disappears as fast as it came.

"You look pretty great yourself, Michael. So glad that we have a brave Spiderman like you guarding our fair city tonight. You never know what kind of criminals will show up."

Michael dances around the room. Kate follows Granny inside.

"Be right back," Michael sings before running upstairs.

It's Granny's turn to hug me. Kate did the same thing earlier and then Bunny. Now Granny. In some ways, all this love feels suffocating. But what would I do without them? These women are practically my family. They love me no matter what. I can't tell my own mother. She doesn't like Will as it is. The first sight of my shiner, and she'll try to press charges. That wouldn't be good for anyone. Still, she and Dad will be by later to see Michael. I'm not sure how I'm getting out of that meeting aside from wearing a ski mask.

"Oh, honey. He did quite a number on you, didn't he?"

"Does it still look that bad? I tried to conceal it with makeup."

Granny frowns. "It's going to take more than make-up to hide that thing. Kate told me what happened. I'm really sorry for what you're going through."

"Thank you."

"Hunter'll make Will see how things really are. Don't you worry."

Kate smiles and answers my unanswered question. "I'm taking Granny to bingo tonight. Hunter's going to stay with Will and join us later if he can."

"I'm sorry I messed up your plans."

"Hunter will thank you. I don't think he can handle Granny in this getup."

"I'm standing right here, you know. I'm not so old that you can talk about me like I'm not here. Hunter needs to get a set and stop being so squeamish about silly things. This is the best costume I've ever had, and considering what happened with that troublemaker, Gertie Cooper, it's timely." Another smile creeps onto my face. "Besides, you haven't seen the best part."

Granny executes a turn to show me the back of her robe. *Bingo Badass* is stitched in large white letters. A chuckle escapes me. The look of pain on Kate's face makes me want to take it back, but it isn't that easy. Instead of smothering my laughter, it grows until the three of us are laughing together.

"Is it time to trick-or-treat yet?"

Michael's tone gets more insistent each time he asks the question. I got home from the General Store around two-thirty. Michael began crying the second he saw my black eye. I answered all his questions honestly except for the part about the location of the incident. He doesn't need to know Will and I were in bed together. Between Bunny and me, we quickly reassured him and turned his attention to the fact that today is Halloween. I let him dress in his costume as soon as we got home, which may have been a mistake since he's been peppering me with the *Is-it-time-to-trick-or-treat* question ever since.

"It's not dark yet. I told you, it will be at least five-thirty before we go out. It might even be later. It has to be good and dark, so we can use your Spiderman flashlight."

He sighs heavily. "Okay, Mommy." He turns to Granny. "Is Frank dressing up for the party?"

"Frank says he'd rather stay home and pass out candy tonight. I think he just doesn't want to dress up and is being a stick-in-the-mud." She shrugs. "You would dress up if you were my boyfriend, right?"

"Yes, I would."

Granny gives Michael a kiss on the top of his head. "We'd best be going, Kate. We're gonna be late if we don't get a move on."

Kate gives me another hug. "Call me if you hear

anything. Promise?"

"Yeah," I add in a whisper, "Thanks for taking Granny to bingo tonight, so Hunter can help me."

She squeezes my hand. "Anything for you. I love you."

"I love you, too."

"Is it time yet, Mommy?"

I glance out the window to get a measure on the amount of sunshine left for the night. "Getting close, pumpkin. Why don't you go in the kitchen and finish up your chicken tenders and apple slices? By the time you're finished, it should be time to go out trick-or-treating." Michael's face erupts into delight. I turn on my mom voice. "But, make sure you take small bites and chew carefully. If you finish too quickly, then you'll just have to wait."

Michael runs toward the kitchen. He does turn and give me an *Okay, Mommy* before he continues through the doorway that leads to our little kitchen.

The doorbell chimes again. That should be Mom and Dad. Might as well get the black eye discussion going. I'll never be able to explain this to Mom in a way she'll understand. I'm just going to have to tell them the truth about what Will did to give me a black eye. *It was an accident.* How many times am I going to have to utter those words in the next few weeks?

Okay. I can do this. I stand tall and open the door to reveal a full-sized Spiderman. His face is covered with a mask similar to the version that came with

Michael's costume. Yet, this adult version has a creepy factor. The man just stands there. I peek my head out and look around for the child or two that should be with him. He's alone.

Now, it's getting really strange. My own Spidey senses begin tingling. I ignore them. This day has been too weird and crazy. It's Halloween. There are lots of adults in costume. Granny just left my house wearing shorts and boxing gloves around her neck.

"Can I help you?"

He reaches his hands to his neck and pulls his mask off.

Malcolm.

"Trick-or-treat, Melanie."

I move to slam the door. Too late. Malcolm blocks the door with his foot and then shoves his way into the house.

"Get out."

He doesn't. He quietly closes the door behind him.

What the hell?

"Where's Michael?"

"He's not here."

"Of course he's here."

"He's not. He went out with some friends."

I say a silent prayer for Michael to stay in the kitchen or hide, anything to stay away from his father.

Malcolm shakes his head. "No, he didn't. Call him to come down."

I don't dare move. "No. You left us. You made the choice to not be a part of his life."

"Choice? Ha! There was no choice. I was happy. I had sex any time I wanted it. I had a little wifey-poo who cooked, cleaned, and brought home a decent paycheck. That kid came along and screwed up the good thing I had going."

"That's not true."

"Oh, yes. You had to fuck up everything and get pregnant."

"Michael's the best thing in my life. You were the one who screwed up when you left."

"Well, I'm back now. I want my time with my son, and I want my share of his trust fund."

"Is that what this is about? The money Aunt Maggie gave him? That's for Michael's college."

"I want my share. You give it to me, or I'll turn your new lover in for giving you that shiner."

Malcolm's threat has no weight. I have no idea how Malcolm knows Will's responsible for my black eye, but he doesn't seem to realize that Will's already at the police station. I take a deep breath and stand a bit taller.

"That's Michael's money. Not yours."

"I tried to do this the right way. I tried to get you back. I came to see you, I sucked up to your parents, and I even paid for new mulch and for the front door to be painted. I wanted you to see that I was serious and back for good." I'm in such shock at his speech that words don't come out. I shake my head from side to side. "That's fine. If you won't take me back, then I'll just take Michael with me."

"No."

Malcolm smiles eerily and turns his body toward the stairs. "Michael, where are you buddy?"

The reality of my situation crashes down on me. There's no way I'm letting Malcolm kidnap my son.

"Hide Michael. Don't..." the words don't make it out before Malcolm shoves into my chest, knocking me to the ground. I can't breathe. "No." The word comes out as a squeak.

I push against him. My movements feel as if they're in vain, but I push harder.

Malcolm's hand comes down hard against my cheek.

There's only black.

Chapter Thirty

Will

"Let's go!"

Hunter runs into the room and quickly unlocks my jail cell. His body is practically vibrating with energy. What does this mean?

"Where are we going?"

"It's Melanie." That's all I need to hear. Something's wrong, and it's serious. Hunter breaks out in a run, and I follow him out the front of the police station. We jump into his Jeep.

"What's happening?"

"I don't know exactly. A call came in from Bunny. Bryce and McMann are on their way to her house, but we're closer."

"Are they hurt? Michael? Melanie? Aunt Bunny?"

"Maybe. I...I don't know. An ambulance has been called as well."

Hunter presses harder on the gas. The entire trip couldn't take more than a few minutes at this speed. Still, it's the longest ride of my life. Once Hunter turns off the main street, he can't drive fast due to the trick-or-treaters and their parents on the sidewalks. Michael was so excited for Halloween.

Please let them be okay.

Hunter pulls over to the side of the road in front of Bunny's house.

Malcolm stands on her porch beating on the front door and shouting. I jump from the Jeep, run across the yard, and climb the front steps just as Malcolm slams one of the metal chairs against a window. Glass shatters. There's no way I'm letting that asshole get inside Aunt Bunny's house.

I grab his arm and turn him to face me. His eyes widen at the sight of me.

"Malcolm Blackstone, you are under arrest." Hunter's voice is all business.

Malcolm launches his fist in my direction, but I easily avert his punch. My fist connects with his chin, and he's down. Hunter quickly handcuffs him before he even realizes what happened.

I jump through the broken window and into the living room.

"Aunt Bunny? Where are you?" She isn't in the living room or dining room. I hear the sound of footsteps overhead and run back toward the front of the house and the staircase.

My eyes meet Michael's at the top of the staircase. He runs down as I run up, and we meet in the middle. I pull him to me in a tight hug. He's okay. Aunt Bunny appears at the top of the staircase. The worry in her eyes practically stops my heart from beating. This isn't over.

"Where's Melanie?"

"At her house," Aunt Bunny practically shouts. "Go."

I set Michael down on the stairs as carefully and quickly as I can.

"A man hit Mommy."

"Show me." I manage to keep my words calm for Michael, despite the loudness of the blood rushing through my body. I have to keep it together.

I run down the few remaining steps, out the front door, and across the yard to Melanie's open front door. A siren cuts through the night.

Oh, Melanie.

She lies on the floor. Her chest rises and falls with her breaths. She's unconscious. *Thank you, Lord, she's not dead.* Melanie's not in good shape.

Melanie's mother kneels beside her. Melanie's father rushes in from the kitchen. "Michael! Thank God you're okay." He pulls Michael to him for a hug. "What happened?"

"A mean man did this to Mommy."

Mr. Woodside releases Michael and kneels down

next to his wife at Melanie's side.

Michael and I take the other side. I squeeze Melanie's hand gently. Michael places his hand over our clasped ones. I wrap my free arm around Michael's shoulders and pull him to me.

Poor Melanie. She now has two black eyes. Her nose is pushed to the side—definitely broken.

Please, Melanie. Please be okay.

The paramedics rush inside the house and push us away from her. We watch them work. I want to know more about what happened, but all I can do is watch the men work on Melanie.

Michael clings to me during the entire process. I know someone should take him to the other room so he doesn't have to watch this. I can't leave. Apparently, the Woodsides can't either. We're all transfixed by the scene before us.

Melanie's eyes flutter open.

"Mommy!" Michael scoots close to her head so she can see him.

Melanie doesn't speak, but her mouth moves as if she's trying to form words or at least a smile. Her eyes close. Michael returns to my side as the paramedics lift Melanie onto a stretcher. Mrs. Woodside and I look at each other with the unspoken question of who is going to ride in the ambulance with Melanie.

Mrs. Woodside gives me a small smile. "You go. Michael, John, and I will meet you at the hospital."

"Thank you."

The two small words don't convey how thankful I really am. Gratitude wells up inside me. I know this was a big step for her. I truly am so thankful.

I kneel down again so I'm eye-to-eye with Michael. "You go with your grandma. I will see you at the hospital, okay buddy?"

Michael squeezes my neck tightly and turns to his grandmother. I follow the emergency workers and Melanie to the ambulance. We get settled inside. I get the seat next to Melanie, and I hold her hand the entire way to the hospital.

Chapter Thirty-One

Melanie

Who's pounding?

I never get to take a nap, and when I finally do, someone is banging with a hammer.

Can't be a hammer. The bam-bam-bam is too precise. More like throbbing.

Uh. It's my head.

A jolt of pain mows through my head and down my spine. A moan escapes from my dry lips.

My eyes open. I blink a few times to help my vision clear.

"Will." The word is barely a whisper. He leans over me and smiles.

Will's here with me. A tear rolls down my cheek.

Is it because Will came back to me or because of the relentless pounding? It's followed by another. Will leans closer and kisses them away.

"Michael?"

"Michael's okay, sweetheart. He's just outside in the waiting room with your parents." My relief comes out in a quick breath. "I'm so sorry I left you. If I'd been there, this wouldn't have happened."

I swallow hard to choke back the threatening tears. I have to concentrate on talking right now. I don't want to waste my energy on crying.

"Malcolm wanted to take Michael from me. He tried to kidnap him for his inheritance."

"Malcolm won't hurt you ever again. He's going to jail."

"What happened?"

"Michael's the hero of the day."

"My baby."

Will smiles. "Michael was in the kitchen when Malcolm arrived. He overheard what was happening and ran out your back door and over to Aunt Bunny's house. She called the police." There's no stopping the tears now. I begin crying in earnest. "Hunter and I rushed to the scene and found Malcolm trying to get inside Bunny's house. Bunny and Michael were locked in her bedroom upstairs. We got there just in time. He's in jail now."

I take another deep breath. "Malcolm was acting totally crazy."

"Malcolm told Hunter he heard about your aunt's

passing. He saw an opportunity to get some of the money. I'm sorry."

"He wanted to steal from his son. That makes no sense. Maybe it's my concussion. I know I have one. What else is wrong with me?"

"You now have two black eyes and a broken nose." My hand flies to my face. I wince as it comes in contact with my bandaged nose. "They reset it and say it'll be as good as new." Will brings his hand to my face. He gently caresses my jawline. He sighs. "I'm sorry I hurt you this morning."

"It wasn't your fault."

"It was in a way. I know I can be dangerous while I'm sleeping. When I'm with you, I feel better than I have in ages. I was being selfish to put you in that position."

"No. I want to be with you. It'll get better. It already has."

"I'm staying." I try to smile. I'm not sure I pull it off—the movement feels clumsy. "I'm not leaving you again unless you ask me to, and that would break my heart. I love you, Melanie, and I love Michael, too."

"I will never ask you to leave. I love you."

Will moves closer and plants a feather-light kiss on my lips.

"Mommy?"

Michael steps cautiously into my room and climbs into Will's lap. Tears threaten again, but this time happy tears, as I watch the two of them together. This is what family is supposed to be.

"I'm going to be okay, pumpkin. You're my hero, you know."

"I know. Uncle Hunter gave me this cool badge."

Sure enough, Michael has a plastic police badge pinned to his Spiderman costume.

"Can I speak with you a minute, Mel?"

Mom. She and Dad step into the room.

"Let's go tell everyone that your Mommy's awake."

"Who else is here?"

"Everyone in town—that I know, anyway. Aunt Bunny, Hunter, Kate, Brady, their parents, Bryce, Frank, and Granny. It's quite a crowd."

Will gives me another smile, stands up, and carries Michael out of the room.

Dad puts his hand on my forearm and squeezes. "We were so scared when we found you like we did. If we'd only arrived a little earlier."

"This isn't your fault. Malcolm's crazy."

"I love you, honey."

"Love you, too, Daddy."

He walks out of the room, leaving me alone with my mom. I haven't been thrilled with her lately because of the shots she's taken at Will. That's forgotten in this moment when I see the sadness in her eyes. She reaches for my hand.

"I owe you an apology."

"It's okay."

"It's not okay. I was pushing you toward Malcolm

when I should have known better. I was so angry at him for leaving you and Michael. Yet, I believed him when he said he wanted a second chance. He's Michael's father. I just thought it would be so much simpler if the three of you could all be a family." She takes a deep breath and lets it out slowly. "Life isn't always simple. I should know that after all these years." A tear falls down her cheek. "I didn't give Will a chance. I thought you were clinging to him to help save him."

"Mom."

"You do have a tendency to want to take care of everyone. I didn't want you to repeat past mistakes there, but I was totally wrong. Will's a wonderful man. He'll be a great father for Michael, and he loves you."

He does love me.

"Thank you, Mom."

"We've taken up enough of your time. Get some sleep, honey."

Epilogue

Melanie

"Such great news from Dr. Hanover."

I whisper the words as I find Kate sitting in the rocking chair at her mom's bedside. She texted me from the waiting room as soon as they got word about Grace's surgery. It was a huge success in that the cancer hadn't spread from her ovaries. Her chances of beating the cancer are now ninety-five percent in her favor.

Kate stands and meets me halfway for a hug. She looks like she's been pulled through the ringer. Her clothes are wrinkled, and there are bags under her eyes.

"We're all so happy with the outcome. Dr. Hanover says Mom should get to go home tomorrow. She'll have some chemo but not a lot. It's really only preventative, just to make sure the cancer is really gone. He thinks they got it all during the surgery."

Tears fill my eyes as we watch Grace sleep. This woman is almost like a mom to me. We were hopeful about the surgery, but as the procedure got closer, our stress grew. Luckily, it's only been a little over a month since I ran into Grace and Albert in the hospital and learned she had cancer. The quick action of Dr. Hanover certainly helped.

"You look exhausted. Why don't you go home and get some rest?"

"I will soon. Hunter's coming to keep me company after he closes up the store at eight. Brady'll be here after Mayfair closes. He's taking the overnight shift. Dad was a mess. We made him go home a little while ago."

"I know you've been through a lot today, but can you help me with something?"

"Of course. Anything."

I hold up the box for Kate to see. Her eyes widen with surprise.

"Are you pregnant?"

"I don't know. I think so, but I'm scared to take the test."

She wraps her arm around my shoulders and squeezes gently. "This is great. Will loves you so much. He'll be thrilled to have a baby with you."

I know. *I think.* Almost every part of me agrees with Kate's statement. Will says he loves me, and I feel like he loves me. It's just that we've only been together a month, barely enough time to even get pregnant. Yes, I know it only takes one time, and we've had sex way more than that, but did I not learn anything from my experience with Malcolm? With Malcolm, we'd been married for five months, and it wasn't enough time.

"Will's not Malcolm. This could be great news. We'll be pregnant at the same time just like we always talked about when we were younger."

Okay. I've been thinking about this all day. I can't delay any longer. "I'll be right back."

I step into the bathroom, do what I need to do, and set the stick on the counter to wait. There's a light knock on the door. Kate steps inside without even waiting for a response. She takes my arm, and we stare at the test together. Just waiting. Waiting more as the pale blue slowly takes over the little window. This has to be the longest two minutes of my life. Kate lets out a small squeal of excitement. I see it, too.

Two blue lines.

I'm pregnant.

The pounding of my heartbeat echoes in my ears. The little lines become blurry. I wipe the tears from my eyes, and the test comes back into focus. Kate pulls me to her and rubs my back.

"It's going to be fine, great even. You have nothing to worry about." What if it isn't? "Where's Will now?"

"He's at home with Michael. Will picked him up from preschool today and made him dinner."

"Go. Tell. Him." Kate's right. I have to tell him.

The ride home gives me time to think. All day I

worried about what the test result would be. Now that I know I'm pregnant, and the unknown is out of the equation, I feel better. It was such an emotional day with Grace's surgery, Ellen's resigning, and me wondering if I might be pregnant. Way too much for one day.

Somehow, the anxiety dissipates as I get closer to home. Yes, I would be devastated if Will left me, but he won't. I know he won't. If he did, I would have another baby to raise by myself. I push the thought out of my head. It won't happen that way.

Things have been amazing between us. Will's feeling better and better each day. He still won't let himself sleep in the same bed with me, but his nightmares are getting fewer and fewer as time goes on. Will says I'm the one responsible for the improvement in his health. Maybe that's part of it, but it's more than just our relationship. Will spends most of the day writing. He's working on a military thriller. Writing has proven to be cathartic for him as is spending time with Michael. Will has always been relaxed around Michael and his friends. Will likes children.

This is going to be fine.

I repeat that mantra the whole way home.

Michael meets me with a hug as soon as I enter the house. He's fresh from his bath and eager to tell me about his day. Will plants a welcome home kiss on my cheek. I feel his eyes studying me as Michael explains the science project they did in school today.

Something with marshmallows and pasta. I can't concentrate on his words since I can't stop thinking about my own news.

"Michael, why don't you go upstairs and draw a picture of what your marshmallow sculpture looked like?"

"Good idea," he says excitedly as he runs up the stairs.

Will comes to my side immediately. "Did you get bad news about Grace? I thought her surgery went well."

I guess there's no putting this off, not that I could if I wanted to.

"Grace is great, but I do need to tell you something." I glance at the staircase knowing that Michael is in his room but still close enough to overhear. "Let's go into the kitchen. I don't want Michael to hear."

Will follows me and turns me to face him as soon as we get through the door.

"What is it? You're scaring me."

"I hope not. It's just that I'm...pregnant."

I watch Will's face as he processes my words. First disbelief. His mouth opens in surprise. Then it happens. He lets out a whoosh of breath.

"You're pregnant?"

I bite my lip and nod, still not sure where this is going.

"We're going to have a baby?"

I nod again, this time faster. His eyes begin to

tear up. A tear slides down my own cheek, although I'm not sure yet if it's a happy tear or a sad one. I'm too much of an emotional mess to know.

Will hugs me to him and spins me around.

He's practically dancing around the kitchen just like I always hoped, and he's laughing. *Laughing*. A breath that I didn't even realize I was holding is released. The tears fall freely now. He stops turning. Our eyes meet.

"This is the best news." I let my forehead fall to meet his. I want to take in and feel this moment forever "You were biting your lip when you told me. Were you worried?"

"I was. I wasn't sure how you'd take the news."

"Don't ever doubt how much I love you, Melanie Woodside. I can't wait to tell everyone I know. I'm going to be a dad." Tears are falling again. Will wipes them from my cheeks. "Maybe I can tell everyone I'm going to be a husband, too. Will you marry me, Mel?"

"Of course I will." I choke out the words between sobs.

"Aunt Bunny will be beside herself. She planned for us to get together, you know."

A chuckle escapes me. "Of course she did. I shouldn't be surprised."

"I need to thank her. Without her guidance, fate might not have led me here, and this is exactly where I'm supposed to be."

Dear Reader,

I hope you enjoyed *Guiding Fate*. If so, please consider writing an online review. Reviews are very helpful and would be very much appreciated.

If you would like to be notified of upcoming releases, please sign up for my newsletter at www.tamralassiter.com. I'd also love to connect with you on Twitter or Facebook.

Sincerely,

Tamra Lassiter

Trusting Fate (***Role of Fate*** Book 5)
Coming Fall 2016

Other titles in the *Role of Fate* series:
Deciding Fate (Book 1)
Blinding Fate (Book 2)
Creating Fate (Book 3)

Romantic Suspense:
No More Regrets
Perfectly Innocent
Something to Lose
I Take Thee to Deceive
Favorable Consequences

Young Adult Fantasy:
The Gifted

Acknowledgements

There are some people you meet in life that you just know are incredible souls. Dicey "June" Kuhne is one of these people. She's been with our family through good times and bad times. With June, we have gotten my mother unstuck from a blow-up obstacle course, eaten our first buttermilk pie, and taken a Hummer limo to Krispy Kreme. The woman is up for anything, and that's just one of the things I love most about her. Thank you, June, for always being such a generous and supportive friend!

Thank you also to Jen Rzepka, Pat Williams, Anne Newport, Suzanne Bhattacharya, and all the Team Tamra members who helped me with little decisions throughout the writing of this book!

Special thanks to Mary McGahren for the incredible cover. I love these Role of Fate covers!

Thanks to Jena O'Connor of Practical Proofing, Toni Metcalf, and Mary Featherly for all your help with editing and proofing.